Echelon Press

Wyrd Wravings

An anthology of humorous speculative fiction

Margaret Bailey	Lynn David Hebert
Ellen Dawn Benefield	Kfir Luzzatto
Linda DeMeulemeester	Janet Miller
Karen Duvall	Candace Sams
Lazette Gifford	Marc Vun Kannon

Echelon Ensign

Echelon Press

Crowley, Texas

Echelon Press
P.O. Box 1084
Crowley, TX 76036

Echelon Ensign
First paperback printing: September 2003

ISBN 1-59080-264-0

Printed and bound in the United States of America

www.echelonpress.com

Table of Contents

A Measly Bottle of Oxygen

Margaret Bailey

A Measly Bottle of Oxygen

Melvin Bledsoe stood at a boardwalk intersection in Greenland International Preserve in September of 2183, sweating in the unconditioned heat and feeling more uneasy than he had in years. Before him stood a pole bristling with arrows and enigmatic names. He checked the sign post for a small computer screen to inform him where to go next. There wasn't even an icon to click. How was he supposed to decide where to go? He put his hands on his ample hips and shook his head over the shoddy lack of information. The last park in the world, and he couldn't even make data entry out of the signs.

He glanced around at the walkways through the greenery and shuddered. If this was "nature as it once was," he was glad it had changed. All this walking around in the open. It was too unsettling, such huge space with no oxygen mask. And way too green. And then there was the air. True, it wasn't sluggish like the plant enhanced air of his apartment, but it lacked the invigorating bite of the air from the tanks. It was bland, hardly noticeable, in fact, and made him anxious.

A group of Cauc/Asian girls stopped at the sign, chattering away in their hybrid language, clearly delighted with the park. One of them glanced up at his grotesque height, nudged several others, and pointed at him. They giggled.

Melvin turned away, conscious of being among the homeliest of the twelve and a half billion men of his time. He ran his hand over the short black hair receding above his temples, simultaneously hiding his most embarrassing feature, his eyebrows. The hairs in his eyebrows grew laterally between his nose and a point roughly above his pupils. There they turned upwards, like little black horns. The left one was hyperactive, and he knew it gave his face an evil sarcasm that turned people away.

Lonely and indecisive, he studied the sign again until a voice at his elbow startled him. He looked down at a woman he'd seen at the visitors' compound and taken for some exotic Greenland native, a kind of pixie. She stood slightly taller than his elbow and her slender frame radiated energy. Her dark red hair leapt from her head as an uncontrollable mop of curls. Her face had the pallor typical of the 2180's, but her green eyes were full of laughter. Her mouth was so mobile Melvin was unable to define it.

"...heard of trees," she was saying, "but I never dreamed they would be so big. Can you imagine what it must have been like before they had to reservoir air and water? Have you seen the trees in any of the climate bubbles, like the ones with the needles on them, or the ones that turn red?"

She didn't stop, but he couldn't keep up with her. He'd never known anyone to go on this way.

"...remember hearing about the forests in the dorm school? Did you know they used to build with trees? Like this very walkway we're on!" She ran her hand along the gray-brown railing. "Feel this. You suppose it's actually wood? Have you been to the section with the flowering trees?"

Melvin was dumbstruck. She wasn't even remotely concerned about air consumption.

"My name's Alwyn," she said. "What's yours?"

"Melvin. Melvin...uh...Bledsoe." He felt his eyebrow hit turbo, but all she did was glance up at it and grin.

"Where are you from?" she asked.

"New City Denco 5," he managed to say without stammering.

"No!!" It was a verbal explosion accompanied by a bulging of eyes and two steps backwards. "I'm from Denco 4! This is too much. I can't believe we came all the way to Greenland to meet like this. What floor do you live on?"

"Hundred seventeen," said Melvin, not without some pride.

Alwyn backed away again. "You're that important?"

Feeling his face redden, Melvin looked down past his pear-shaped mid-section. "I don't know how important..."

"Oh, yeah, you are. I only live on eighteen, but I've seen those uppers," she said. "You can work in them all day with no air tank or anything. Nobody gets them but IRS or PIA big-guys." She set one foot behind the other, as if ready to turn and run.

Melvin nearly gave up on the conversation. But there was something about this woman, almost as captivating as a computer fantasy. As if free air were her natural element. He tried to draw her back. "Well, of course, I can't leave home without a tank, just like everybody else."

Alwyn stared at him.

Melvin could almost see decision wheels turning behind her eyes. He wanted to say something more, but nothing came to mind. Knowing she'd turn away now and stung by the rejection, he fled mentally to the comforting closeness of his apartment, with its three life-sustaining walls, completely lined with flowerless plants genetically engineered for high efficiency oxygen production. They shone dully in the constant electric light but made the apartment dark and muggy.

In one wall was his small window, which had looked on the ancient city of Denver during its great years.

The fourth wall housed his International Respiratory Service hook-up for supplementary breathable gases and the computer that served as office, library, bank, and personal enrichment center. In surround realism it provided him with experiences that ranged from space travel to warfare, from poetry to the most ravishing sexual fantasies. His computer assumed so many of the basic necessities that he often didn't leave the apartment for weeks at a stretch. But that was home. Not this unsettling open place with a babbling sprite who was still giving him a speculative look.

Alwyn's eyes narrowed and she said, "You IRS or PIA?"

"International Respiratory Service," he said. "I'm an accountant. I've never worked for the Plant Inspection Agency."

She stepped closer again and raised one hand to hide her mouth from onlookers. "Consider yourself lucky," she said in a half whisper. "I don't like those guys at all. Poking around in other people's personal plants. Handing out fines for negligence or sending them back to the Old City dorms. They're a mean lot." She took her hand down and perched on the railing. "Speaking of which, who's minding your plants for you?"

"My neighbor, Roman," said Melvin, stunned that she was still here. "What about yours?"

Alwyn looked away. "Oh... That's been taken care of. Listen, have you been to any of the flower houses yet? No?" She swung off the railing and grabbed his hand. "Come with me. It'd be a crime to go back to Denco without seeing a single flower. When are you going back, anyway? I'm going back the day after tomorrow, but I wish I could stay. I just love it here, don't you? I haven't spent this much time without an oxygen tank—ever. And all these plants that no one altered genetically. I think it's fascinating."

Melvin was mesmerized. For the next two days they visited every exhibit in the park. Through her eyes he saw the old natural wonders in an entirely new glow of delight. He followed the chattering, colorful pixie through an enchanted landscape without registering half of what she said, oblivious of the more economical conversations around them, simply grateful not to be alone.

She left Greenland two days ahead of him and they agreed to meet at his apartment on the evening of his return. In his last days there, which he spent mooning about in fantasies that rivaled his computer, a nagging thought, a kind of suspicion, kept trying to surface. Each time, he slapped a daydream over it and counted the hours until their date.

* * *

His fingerprint on the sensor-lock opened his door; he stepped into his apartment and took off his oxygen mask. What greeted him so shocked him that he staggered backwards. All three of his plant walls were brown. Limp. Dead.

"Holy Ozone!" he whispered, dropping his oxygen bottle on his right foot. He rushed to the tap that ran water into the troughs, but the exertion made him dizzy in the airless room. He started to put his oxygen mask back on but remembered how little was left in the tank, ran instead to the IRS hook-up and pushed a button. The screen on the monitor flashed EMERGENCY.

Immediately air streamed into his face and he inhaled deeply. He rushed to his window, holding his breath. Perhaps other apartments on his level had died. He pushed the drooping leaves aside and wiped a swath across the grimy glass. All the other windows were ringed by healthy green. Briefly, he wondered whether anyone had noticed his window and notified the PIA. He turned from the window, expelling the breath he was holding. There was no more air coming from the vent. He hit the emergency button again.

EMERGENCY ALLOTMENT 4 CONSUMED, the monitor informed him.

Melvin was near panic, his eyebrow in perpetual motion. He pushed the 6 button, which would normally give him enough oxygen for the light exercise people occasionally did. That might give him enough for a couple of hours. The monitor flashed

PLANT MALFUNCTION.

SUSPECTED NEGLIGENCE.

ALLOTMENT 3 ALLOWED.

ONE PERSON.

NO HEAVY BREATHING.

The "heavy breathing" brought him up short. He'd forgotten his date with Alwyn. He forced himself to be calm, pulled his eyebrow down unconsciously, went back to the oxygen vent, breathed slowly a few times, and tried to organize his thoughts. For the first time he remembered Roman, who'd promised to keep an eye on his plants. Grabbing his mask and tank, he rushed out into the narrow hall to the next door. At his banging the door opened enough for him to see it was a woman.

Melvin was stunned. "Where's Roman?"

"Who's Roman?" she countered.

"Holy green, the man who lives here, of course!"

She narrowed the opening until only one eye glared out at him. "I live here. I think he died about 10 days ago," she said.

"Had a bad respiratory attack when his hook-up malfunctioned or something."

Melvin felt his eyebrow shoot up to his hairline, and the woman slammed the door. His brain reeled. His very life was in danger, his only friendly neighbor was dead, he had his first and probably only chance to be friends with a real woman, and it was all ruined because of the stupid plants. Breath or no breath, plants were nothing but trouble.

"CFC," he swore under the mask as he slammed his door. He would have to call Alwyn. Not that he dared tell her what had happened. He would try to go to her place instead. But when he dialed her his monitor showed

DISCONNECTED.

His sister Annie. She would help.

Annie, being as infelicitous a combination of genes as her brother, never turned on her pictaphone. "Oh, hi, Mel. I thought you were off on vacation," she said.

"I was, but when I got back all my plants were dead."

Annie gasped and appeared on the monitor simultaneously. "Get away from the camera so I can see," she said. "I don't believe you."

Melvin shifted aside, took a few deep breaths at the vent, and returned.

Annie's face, with her bulging eyes and wiry hair, always looked astonished. At the sight of Melvin's dead walls, she looked as if she'd narrowly missed being electrocuted.

"My green, Melvin, you're in deep CFC," she said, a hush in her voice. "How could you let that happen?"

"I didn't <u>let</u> it happen, but I don't have time to explain now. I desperately need some plants in here. I've got a date coming."

"A what?!"

"Very funny. Look, I'm only getting a three allotment from the IRS. Can you bring me some plants and let me have a few cuttings to get me started again?"

"Sorry, bub. The PIA inspected me twice this month. I'm nearly on their most-negligent list now. If I get caught they'll be in my troughs every two days. Why don't you get some from Roman?"

"No dice, there's someone new living there and I don't think I made a good impression on her. I know someone in the next building. Maybe I could borrow some, but he lives down on twenty or thirty."

"That'll never do," said Annie. "You bring those plants up to your level and they'll die in an hour, even if they survive the outside transfer. Look, maybe..."

The buzzer sounded.

"Nuclear Waste!" cried Melvin. "That's got to be Alwyn. Think of something and call me back." He pressed the door release for the first floor. He had three minutes before the solar powered elevator reached the 117th floor.

Melvin tried the emergency button again. The monitor flashed:

EMERGENCY STATUS ALREADY IN EFFECT

WARNING: EMERGENCY ALLOTMENT 3 DISCONTINUES IN 8 MINUTES.

PREPARE FOR ALLOTMENT 2.

SLEEP.

He checked his tanks, hoping desperately that memory didn't serve and that he hadn't planned to replace them all at the Federal Reserve Oxygen Bank when he got back from Greenland. The bottle he'd come home on had about two hours in it. He would meet Alwyn at the elevator and suggest that they go to her place. He'd have to think of something plausible when she asked why.

She knocked. He grabbed his mask and opened the door.

Alwyn pushed in, threw off the mask she was wearing, and grabbed his. Her face was blue. She took three large gasps. Her face nearly returned to its normal pallor, and she said, "Can you lend me a tank? I've been living from tank to tank for two days!"

"What?! Don't you have any oxygen at your place? Where are your extra tanks?"

Alwyn registered the dead walls. "Pollution and contamination!" she swore, grabbing the mask for another gulp.

Melvin recoiled before her strong language, took his mask back, and looked at the dial on the tank. She'd used a full four minutes for those huge gulps. If Alwyn was using the bottle too, especially at the rate she was going, they had less than an hour.

"What on this dying earth is going on, Alwyn? I don't have any air here. I didn't want to leave full tanks...too many break-ins...accident with plants." The last part was barely audible. Melvin grabbed the mask.

"Never heard of *this kind of* accident," she said. "...you have friends...visit? I used up...everybody."

Melvin gave her back the mask. "My sister...in trouble with the PIA. Be quiet, let me think." He put the mask back to his face.

"Got to get a tank," she said, panic rising in her already shrill voice. "Oxygen outlet...neighbors." She began turning blue again.

Melvin handed her the mask.

"Don't you have any friends in this building?" she asked.

"People don't like lending oxygen. Maybe one of us, but two? Be quiet and let me think," he said more forcefully.

Alwyn stared at him from behind the mask.

He took a turn at it and said, "We have to go to the surreallie."

Alwyn exploded. "Surreallie?! Are you off your eco-system? Nobody's gone to surreallies since 2150..."

Melvin clamped the mask over her mouth. With the air from the last gulp he explained, "Surreallie theater has a tankless section. Just hope the air delivery still works. Sit there till we figure...." He grabbed the mask and took such a gulp that the needle on the meter jumped.

"Right," said Alwyn, already pulling him through the door. They shared the oxygen awkwardly, without talking, all the way down and across the pavement to the entrance of the Denco 5 center, where the old theater was.

* * *

The price of admission to the empty surreallie had stunned them, but already there was air streaming through the vents in couple capsule 1, visible as a small swirl of dust in its dim light.

Melvin raised the dome of the clear plastic capsule, they both collapsed onto the double-wide seat, and he lowered the dome again. Oblivious of the dust and of each other, they leaned back in the seat and breathed extravagantly for five full minutes, Melvin in great sighs of relief, Alwyn in quick, desperate gasps. The old screen at the front lit up for a moment and died, but they hardly noticed.

"I can't believe this is happening to me," Melvin said at last.

"I can believe it's happening to _me_. I always seem to be getting into some kind of scrape or other. My last boss said I was a throwback and would never fit into our time. When I won the drawing and got that trip to Greenland, he made me quit. He was so mad. He said I'd probably never come back from Greenland anyway."

"You won a prize? I thought you'd gotten the trip as an award, like I did."

"No, I never said it was an award." She laughed. "An award is the last thing I'd ever get. Or if they ever gave me any recognition for my work, it'd probably be by sending me to that penal moon. Anyway, my prize couldn't have come at a better time—just two days before my eviction went into effect."

"You got evicted?! Why?" Melvin whispered. He recoiled from her as far as his round hips and the confines of the capsule would permit.

Alwyn's face reddened. "I know, I should've told you. And since I got back I've been visiting all the people I know, borrowing oxygen tanks that were nearly empty anyway. I even got one from my old boss when he wasn't looking. It was practically half full and almost made up for his making me quit my job."

"What job?"

"Well, they tried to train me as a root specialist—they thought that would get me away from the temptation to talk so much. But it turned out I'm allergic to practically every known fertilizer. So they gave me a job as plant inspector." She laughed up at him. "Yeah, pretty ironic, me, a plant inspector. I was in the lower levels, heavy duty, you know. But all the people whose plants I inspected complained that I talked too much and they had to raise their air intake after I left. I just can't help it. I love talking to people. Even when they're not very interesting, they still have feelings. And sometimes they really open up."

The thought of her opening him up scared him into pressing closer to the capsule. And yet, something in him wanted her to—a thought too frightening to pursue. "Why did you get evicted?"

"Oh, it was so stupid of me. I should have known it wouldn't work. They found out I was using the wrong name."

She drew both feet up on the seat and faced him. "Aren't you uncomfortable squashing yourself into the corner like that? I have plenty of room. How do you do that with your eyebrow?"

Melvin felt his face go hot. It was the first time in years he'd completely forgotten his stupid eyebrow and the first time in his life that anyone had referred to it so directly. He put his hand up, yanked it into place, and held it. "I guess it's a nervous tic I have," he said. "I can't control it. Whenever anything happens to me, it just shoots up. I know it looks awful."

She cocked her head to the right. "You think so? I think it's interesting. Nobody's ever reacted to me that way before, and I've gotten some weird reactions. Anyway, this apartment was one I had inspected, and I knew the person in it was being given one higher up. And I also happened to know the woman who was next in line for a higher room, so when the two things fell together, I went to the new city housing service and said I was the woman who was next in line. I was so tired of that dormitory in the old city. Not that I minded all the people being around. They just wouldn't talk to me any more. Especially the men. They weren't interested in sharing oxygen with me unless...well, you know."

"Unless what?...Oh, yeah, I see. You think it's interesting?" he asked from behind his hand.

"What?"

"My...uh...eyebrow."

"Oh, sure. Almost like real air. It's so different."

Melvin relaxed a little from the capsule wall, which caused his right hip to touch Alwyn's drawn up knees. She didn't move. He relaxed some more.

"You can take your hand down, Melvin. I don't care if your eyebrow does a native rain dance like the one we saw in Greenland."

Tentatively, Melvin lowered his arm, prepared to grab his eyebrow again if necessary. Alwyn took his hand. The eyebrow hit his hairline.

"It's okay, really, Mel. It's nice to know you react to me at all. And since you're not too verbal, it's a great signal."

Melvin smiled. How long had it been since he'd done that? And the feel of her hand on his...

"So anyway, I moved into the apartment. I almost went crazy at first with no one to talk to at all. I started visiting everybody I knew, but I could tell they weren't really glad to see me. I went through so many oxygen tanks that I was down to my last tank long before the end of every refill period." A guilty look passed across her face and she shrugged. "I'm afraid I neglected my plants, too. Can't you just see the reaction at the PIA—a plant inspector who neglects plants? And then one day I got inspected by a man I used to work with. I guess he gave me the ax." She actually paused. "Sometimes I wish I'd been born in the nineteenth instead of the twenty-second century. Did they?..."

"I'm glad you were born in my time," Melvin interrupted, not giving himself a chance to think about what he was saying.

She gave him a wry little smile. "Aw, thanks, Mel."

"'Did they' what?"

"Did they ever tell you what it was like back then, with the families and the parties and conversations just for fun?"

"Yeah, but I didn't believe much of it. Or maybe I just couldn't imagine it. Like forests. All that green stuff outside and no masks." Suddenly a realization hit him. "So when you met me in Greenland, I guess you just saw me as a potential source of oxygen." The insight was very bitter.

"Well, I have to admit, that was partly it."

Shame stabbed his heart, and Melvin yanked his hand away.

"Hey, you didn't let me finish, Mel. It was also because you looked so out of place and unable to enjoy your freedom from the oxygen tank. I loved it so much, those real trees, that sort of blue sky outside the domes, the whole thing. I just couldn't stand seeing anyone *not* enjoying it."

Melvin glanced at her and away. He wanted to run, but there was nowhere to go, even if he could leave her without air.

Alwyn put her hand up to his eyebrow. "Look, Melvin, maybe I am a throwback and some of the awful things people have called me. But if I say I got interested in you for yourself and not for a measly bottle of oxygen, you can believe it. A liar I am not."

He looked again, and her eyes didn't waver from his. Could she really be interested in him? He relaxed his hand so that it was near hers, and she took it in both of hers.

He stared down at their entwined fingers. "Maybe it wasn't the freedom from the oxygen tank I couldn't enjoy," he said. He took a deep breath before he continued. "Maybe I just realized how alone I was...am. I saw all the other people there making friends and having a good time together. And there was me—the eternal outsider." He was admitting this to himself as much as to her, opening up. And she wasn't laughing at him. "And when you came along, I felt like I fit in again."

"Of course," she said. "I know just what you mean. For all my chatter, I've always felt like the odd man out, too."

There was silence. Then she kissed him, and he knew that this hare-brained chatterbox of a throwback to the nineteenth century was going to complicate his life forever.

He laughed. "So when you got to my place and saw all the dead plants...?"

Alwyn grinned. "And I was hoping to stay the night with you."

"The whole night? Two people in one sleeping alcove? I didn't think you could do that."

"You have to put the oxygen on 6 until your breathing goes back to normal. Then you have to be very, very still."

Melvin looked away so as not to betray the jealousy that turned his insides to slime. "You've done this often?"

"Well, no, not often. I guess word got around that being very, very still is not in my nature, and you know how talking uses up the oxygen."

"Yeah," said Melvin, though he didn't know at all. The mention of oxygen consumption brought him back to their present dilemma.

As if she'd read his thoughts, she said, "Melvin, you don't have to feel responsible for me. No one is responsible for anyone else these days. When the air in the capsule runs out, I'll go."

"Don't," he said. "Maybe I'm not responsible for you, but I don't want anything to happen to you, and I certainly can't let you go out there with no tank. Let's see if we can figure out what to do now."

They both sat for several minutes trying to confront the impossibility of the situation. The only sound in the dim, obsolete surrealie was the tiny hiss of the air coming into their capsule.

Alwyn scratched her head through the thick curls. "What can you do about your plants?"

"I already tried everything I could think of. We can forget my apartment for the time being. And I don't think we have much time left in this capsule. Weren't they timed to 45 minutes or something? We can't stay here. We've just got to find some tanks, and I don't think we're going to find any Federal Reserve Oxygen Banks open for at least ten hours."

"We'll have to break into one."

"What?!" yelled Melvin. His whole body flopped and banged into the capsule. "Rob the FROB?! Are you completely contaminated?"

"No, listen, not *rob* it. I cased it out once when I was really short. You know, they have air pumped in there all day. The people who work there have it good. And surely there'd be enough left for us to get by for the night. If we could get in, we could breathe easy."

"Alwyn, will you stop that? Do you know what they do with people who mess with the FROB?"

"Yeah, I do, as a matter of fact. They probably wouldn't do much to you but demote you a few floors. At worst they'd send you back to the old city dorm. But they'd send me to the moon colony. You know, the one by Saturn where they're mining the oxygen-rich ring. They say you can walk around there just like in Greenland. No tank or anything. Maybe it wouldn't be so bad..." She trailed off in a speculative fantasy.

Melvin was quiet, busy with his own thoughts. It was clear there was no legal way they could get any air before their supply ran out. But the FROB! She was right about his punishment—losing his job and going back to the dorms. All those people who backed away from him. All those *people*. And if they sent her to the moon... Suddenly his life without her was too bleak to contemplate. But the FROB!

He looked at the meter on the top of his bottle. It showed 22 minutes of oxygen left, but as they would both have to use it, there was probably enough for 10 or 11 minutes. "The FROB is a long way," he said. "We'd never make it on the air left in the tank. There must be something closer than that."

Alwyn slapped herself on the forehead. "Of course," she cried. "The used tank depot. It's only a few minutes from here. None of the tanks are ever completely empty, we'd have oxygen to spare. It's not guarded like the FROB proper, and if we got caught, it wouldn't be nearly as serious."

"Okay, as soon as the capsule goes up we'll try it." He paused. His eyebrow twitched. "Uh, Alwyn, I'm really glad we met in Greenland," he stammered. "I've never known anyone like you."

"Oh, Mel," she said, relaxing into the back of the seat. "I'm so relieved you said that. After all, I've done nothing but double your trouble since you got back."

He turned to her, put his hands on her shoulders and was bending toward her when the capsule gave a beep and retreated to the ceiling, creaking as it went. "Don't try to walk fast," he said. "It'll only use up the oxygen faster. You'll have to show me the way. And don't talk. Who knows what we might find when we get there?" He squeezed her shoulders and smiled.

Alwyn nodded and handed him the mask. Together they walked out, the tank between them, now able to alternate breathing without short fits of panic.

Once out of the building Alwyn steered him to the right, across several intersections, and past dozens of buildings of more than 100 stories.

"There," she said, pointing to an old, unmarked building on the other side of the street.

"How do we get in?"

"Small window at the back. Have to break it."

Melvin looked at the meter on the tank, but couldn't read it in the dark. "Maybe three minutes left," he said. "Have to do it right the first time."

"Gotcha."

They went through a narrow alley to the back of the building. Behind the depot was another high rise that had been constructed after private transportation had been banned and the parking lot had become superfluous. In the narrow space between it and the depot there was nothing.

"Radio active contamination!" swore Alwyn. "There used to be a tank truck under that window."

Melvin looked up. The window was too high for him, too. "Let me think."

Alwyn took a breath and said, "I climb on your shoulders, break window, take breath, jump in, find tank with air, open door for you."

Melvin stared at her. "I can't let you risk going in there with no air."

"You got a better plan? Let's not waste air."

"What if there's an alarm?"

"We go on anyway. No choice."

So Melvin knelt on the pavement, Alwyn climbed onto his knees, then sat on his shoulders. The process was not carried out with ease or grace. Melvin tried to stand up, balancing her on his shoulders and keeping hold of the tank. He lost control, wobbled back to the other building, and spun her head into the wall.

"Watch it!"

"Sorry."

Precariously, they made it to the window, Melvin took a gulp and handed the mask and tank up to Alwyn. She breathed in and smashed the window. Instantly the alley reverberated shrilly, lights went on everywhere, and they both expelled the last breath in shock. Alwyn took another, squeezed Melvin's shoulder, and returned the mask. She reached in, unlatched the window and pushed the frame open. Holding onto the ledge, she brought up her left leg and stepped on his ear. His "ow" was lost in the alarm. Awkwardly, she pulled herself through the window.

Disburdened, Melvin took a breath, stretched, and rubbed his ear. Suddenly he was getting no more oxygen from the tank. He stopped breathing and banged on the door, but his knocking was not audible in the siren, even to him.

After what seemed like hours, the door opened and Alwyn was standing there with a tank in hand. Seeing the panic on his face, she grabbed the hose from his tank and fixed it to hers. After he had breathed, she took a gulp herself.

She pulled his head down and shouted in his ear, "A minute or two. Have to find another one."

Before they could begin their search, the siren stopped, the door from the front of the depot banged open and two black-clad IRS agents leapt into the room, holding their guns in front of them. Even unarmed they would have been intimidating in their full-face gas masks. "Throw down that mask!" The rubbery voices were menacing.

Melvin obeyed. Alwyn put both her hands at her sides and stuck her head out a bit.

One of the agents said, "Put your hands at your sides."

The agents gave them masks. Both breathed in eagerly and slumped to the floor. The agents strapped the bottles to their arms, and dragged the bodies to a battery powered van marked IRS USE ONLY.

* * *

When Melvin came to he was lying on his back in a box not quite long enough for his body, his kneecaps squashed by the lid. Directly over his face was a small monitor. It read

SUFFICIENT OXYGEN FOR BREATHING ONLY.

DO NOT MOVE.

He struggled to clear his head. The walls of his box were made of battered but still transparent Plexiglas. To his left he could see another box like his, the fourth down in a stack of which he could not see the bottom. To the right there was another stack. Beyond that his vision was limited, but his impression was of endless stacks of body boxes.

Accustomed as he was to close quarters, this was more than he could bear. Panic shot through him from head to foot, both jammed against the ends of the box. He jerked his right foot and got a jolt of electricity in his ankle. The monitor beeped and now read:

INSUFFICIENT OXYGEN FOR PANIC.

LIE QUIETLY AND BREATHE NORMALLY.

He tried to obey. The unthinkable was happening to him. He was in jail. He was forbidden to move. He missed Alwyn. "Pollution and Contamination!" he swore, straining his head against the Plexiglas.

The monitor beeped and read:

NEXT OFFENSE RESULTS IN TOTAL LOSS OF OXYGEN.

Melvin lay quiet. He noticed a flashing message at the bottom of the screen:

PUSH BUTTON MARKED "AWAKE."

What button? Instinctively, he moved his right hand and found a small keyboard attached to an old fashioned coil wire. In the narrow confines of the box he moved it up onto his chest and nearly went cross-eyed trying to focus on it without moving his head, but he was able to distinguish the AWAKE button. He pushed it, hoping to arouse the attention of anyone at all.

ENTER IDENTITY NUMBER.

Melvin complied with his fifteen digits. Almost immediately came the list of his crimes:

1. PLANT NEGLIGENCE, 1ST DEGREE
2. CARELESSNESS WITH TANK AIR
3. CONSORTING WITH KNOWN AIR PROFLIGATE
4. ATTEMPTED ROBBERY OF TANK DEPOT

PRISONER HAS FOLLOWING CHOICES; ENTER CORRESPONDING NUMBER:

1. GUILTY
2. GUILTY, MERCY OF COURT
3. INNOCENT
4. REQUEST LAWYER

Melvin's head swam. Somewhere to his left he heard banging and screaming. There was a loud beep, the screaming hit a crescendo of panic, then became a choking sound. When that was still, he heard a panel sliding open and a surface sliding out. Shortly thereafter the sliding noises came in reverse and all was quiet. He forced his attention back to the monitor, feeling absolutely powerless. In desperation he punched in 4. The response came instantly.

LAWYERS NOT PROVIDED FOR CRIMINALS CAUGHT IN THE ACT.

GUILTY.

DO YOU WISH TO PLEAD MERCY OF THE COURT? 1 YES 2 NO.

He pressed 1. The monitor instructed:

PRESS CORRESPONDING NUMBER(S)

1. NO PREVIOUS PLANT NEGLECT

2. OXYGEN PRODUCTION JOB OR IRS

3. OTHER

He felt a spark of hope and punched in all three. After a moment the monitor read:

1 AND 2 ACCEPTED.

ENTER ABBREVIATED REASONS FOR 3.

Melvin thought a minute. Then he typed in:

1. TWO-WEEK VACATION, BACK-UP DIED

2. IN LOVE

There was a short pause.

REASON 2 REJECTED.

PLEA BEING PROCESSED.

WAIT.

Melvin almost laughed aloud at the irony of the instruction to wait, but the memory of the sliding noises was fresh enough to stifle the impulse.

The monitor came back on.

REASONS 1, 2, AND 3 (AMENDED) ACCEPTED. PRISONER IS OFFERED   FOLLOWING CHOICES:

1. LOSS OF RANK IN IRS, RETURN TO OLD CITY

2. DEPORTATION TO GEO-OXY 2

ENTER DECISION IN THREE MINUTES

Melvin could not contain himself this time. "Alwyn," he thought. With a cry of triumph he pushed button 2, expecting to be released instantly from his claustrophobia. Instead the monitor registered:

DECISION MADE IN UNDUE HASTE.

CONSIDERATIONS:

1. NO AIR MASKS ON GEO-OXY 2

2. OXYGEN-RICH ATMOSPHERE CAUSES INITIAL DIZZINESS AND VOMITING

3. PROGNOSIS FOR GEO-OXY 2: EXTRACTION OF PURE OXYGEN FOR EXPORT WILL DEPLETE CURRENT SUPPLY BY 2250. IN EFFORT TO TRANSFORM MOON INTO HABITABLE PLANET, ALL PRISONERS REQUIRED TO MAINTAIN AND INCREASE PLANT LIFE SENT WITH THEM ON PAIN OF DEATH.

This gave him something to consider. How he hated plants. Still, even if he'd been allowed to keep his apartment, he'd have been plagued with them for the rest of his life.

4. NO GROUP HOUSING. PRISONERS REQUIRED TO BUILD OWN DWELLING. CO-HABITATION REQUIRED FOR SURVIVAL, OFTEN RESULTS IN OFFSPRING. NO NURSERIES OR SCHOOLS. PARENTING MANDATORY.

This gave Melvin pause in spite of himself. When he was in Greenland, he'd felt utterly lost, cast adrift from the green womb of his apartment. Now he'd have to spend the rest of his life feeling uneasy. And children—a radical and frightening thought. People hadn't raised their own children in family units for decades and he was certain he had no talent for parenting.

And what of Alwyn as a mother? The picture of her with a baby popped into his head, and something melted inside him. It flooded him with insight into the broken continuity of his century, the negation of the function of all men and women since time began. With the realization came the certain knowledge that he needed that function. He would be a father, like the billions of men before him. He would make himself good at it, and he knew with certainty that Alwyn would be a good mother. And that there was no life for him without her.

If she was on Geo-Oxy 2. His heart nearly failed. Had they given her some other choice? Something she might think he'd choose and choose herself, just to be with him? Did she care that much? No matter what he chose now, it was a risk. She was worth the risk of his whole future, but if he landed on the penal moon alone?

His hand shook as he entered 2 again. The monitor instructed:

ENTER FULL NAME(S) OF PERSON(S) TO BE NOTIFIED OF YOUR DECISION

He typed in "Annie Bledsoe, sister," and her fifteen digits. A small puff of air hit his face and he fell asleep.

* * *

When Melvin came to again, he was in a similar coffin-like affair minus the computer. He was instantly awake and aware of intermittent motion. He looked about. To his right he could see only an aluminum wall. To his left a conveyor belt moved coffins like his, all occupied by women. He looked for Alwyn, but as the conveyor belts moved alternately, he kept seeing the same faces. A small loudspeaker beeped in his right ear.

"Attention, prisoners," said a voice. "You will shortly be placed in suspended animation for the transport to Geo-Oxy 2. Upon arrival you will be given orientation and medical care for the adjustment to the oxygen-rich atmosphere. Thereafter you will be required to choose a partner for co-habitation, as prisoners who choose to live alone on the moon rarely survive. You will work with the Interplanetary Oxygen Service in an attempt to turn Geo-Oxy 2 into a permanently habitable planet. Further crimes against plant life will result in death."

Ahead of him he could see the rocket ship looming into the sky. His heart was beating hard. Required to choose a partner... He wanted no one but Alwyn. Whoever else on earth, no on the moon, would want him? Where was she? Now the men's conveyor belt was moving steadily along. He kept his eyes riveted on the women's belt. Finally, a shock of ridiculous, rebellious hair came into view, all red curls in constant motion. She was obviously searching for someone in the men's belt.

A puff of air hit him in the face and he was asleep before she saw him, before he had a chance to register his own joy. His eyebrow never even got in a quiver.

About the Author:

Margaret Bailey is a retired teacher of German living with her husband in the Rockies west of Denver. She has a family of adopted Vietnamese children and through them two wonderful grandchildren and relatives in California, Vietnam, Australia, France, and Canada. Several of her short stories and novels have won prizes or honorable mention in contests in Colorado, Tennessee, and California.

margaretbailey@echelonpress.com

Suki

Ellen Dawn Benefield

.

Suki

"Suki! Suki! Here kitty, kitty. Where are you?"

This was not possible. She had locked the cat in the carrier herself. The carrier was still locked. The cat was gone. Dr. Anna Zanders sighed.

Sidney would have a fit. Her sister was doing her a big favor as it was, providing a home for Suki. Sidney had barely spoken to Anna since their parents were killed in an earthquake several years ago. Sidney shouldn't have to take an unspayed animal. Twice before when she'd made an appointment this had happened. She'd thought Molly had released the cat but this time her daughter was at school.

Anna wished they could take the cat with them. Suki was Molly's love since the day the bi-colored blue-eyed Ragdoll kitten was placed in her arms by her father. Brad died in an accident a week later.

Dear animal-loving, veterinarian Brad. Anna blinked back tears. She would start over in Luna City, the new lunar mining town. Anna had landed a job in the hydroponics department. The only hitch was leaving Suki behind. She'd begged to take her daughter's beloved pet—in vain. No animals were allowed on the lunar rocket.

Anna shook her head. There was no time to get the cat fixed now.

Two hours later Anna was checking her baggage for the flight. Three-year-old Molly sobbed the entire journey from

Sidney's house to the space port. Anna sniffled. She'd cried herself when she left Suki with her sister.

My, her bag felt heavy all of the sudden. Come to think of it, her brother-in-law had commented on it when he put it in her car.

"Your luggage is fifteen pounds overweight, Dr. Zanders," the attendant said.

Molly giggled. Anna looked down and her small daughter and Molly's face sobered, but the impish hint of a smile lingered. She couldn't possibly have sneaked the cat in the suitcase? There wasn't any time Anna hadn't been watching her. Impossible. The scale must be wrong.

"How can that be? I weighed it before we left." Anna opened her suitcase and searched. There wasn't anything in it she hadn't packed herself. The bare necessities. "Weigh it again."

The attendant shrugged and weighed the luggage again. His eyebrows rose in surprise. "Twenty pounds on the nose."

Anna sniffed. "I told you so. Come on, Molly." Anna looked down as she took her daughter's small hand and was surprised to see Molly smiling through her tears.

Suddenly her baggage felt heavy again. Anna started. She thought she heard a faint meow from her suitcase. Impossible. Space jitters. That's all. Just to be sure, Anna stopped and opened the suitcase. It felt lighter as soon as she placed it on its side. She frowned and blinked back tears. A few long white hairs were on her best sweater. Poor Suki. Well, the cat was better off with her sister, surely. Anna shook her head and continued to their shuttle. They'd have to hurry now. No more letting her imagination play with her.

After Anna found their seats and settled Molly down with a doll, she dozed off and dreamed Suki was sitting in her daughter's lap, purring. Anna woke with a start, for a moment she thought she really saw Suki in Molly's lap. Anna blinked. No cat. She shook her head.

It took thirty-six hours to get to the moon and to find their tiny apartment. Anna had no sooner packed their clothes away and glanced about at the sparsely furnished flat, when the door pager beeped.

She opened it a bit wearily. What now?

"Hi. I'm Patty, your neighbor. I brought your magneto boots. You need to get used to them. That's part of the reason the floors are metal underneath. The magnets stick to the floor. Otherwise your daughter might just float away!"

Patty waved her hands around her face as she chattered and laughed, her belly bounced slowly in the low gravity.

"Aren't you a red-haired beauty! I don't know that I need the competition. I came to Luna City to get a man. Did you know the men outnumber the women three to one? You can be middle-aged and overweight like me and still get dates!"

The lights flickered momentarily. Patty gasped.

"Darn rats! They got to the moon somehow and they chew the wiring and everything. I hope they don't shut off the air."

Anna motioned Patty to come in, the door automatically closed behind the older woman. Patty handed her the boots as Molly came swimming through the door into the living room.

"Oh my," Patty giggled. "We'd better get you booted right away or you'll plumb forget how to walk." Patty showed Molly how to lace her boots and Anna followed with her own footwear.

Molly frowned. "They make me stucked to the floor. I want to fly like Peter Pan and Wendy. Suki flies good, too."

Patty giggled.

"Oh, you'll learn to do that at preschool, but you'll have wings. It's part of the exercise program. You have to exercise constantly on the moon to keep from losing your muscles and bone mass. Low gravity, you know, and the food is rationed. That's the only drawback. I've lost forty pounds since I arrived. Everybody wants to dance and fly after work. All that energy." Her hands fluttered about her plump face.

"Everyone walks everywhere. It's too much work on Earth but here it's easy. I can dance all night without my magnetos on. There are good things about being here and here comes one now."

Patty giggled as the door pager pinged. She bounced to the door and opened it.

"My date. Ralph, this is Anna and don't you dare drool over her like that!" Patty stopped giggling.

Anna stiffened. Just what she didn't need. Some tubby old Don Juan bothering her.

Ralph took her hand, stroking it with his thumb.

"Hello, gorgeous. I intend to see more of you."

Then Ralph sneezed loudly. He sneezed again and kept sneezing. Tears ran down his cheeks. He pulled a handkerchief from his pocket and blew his nose.

"I doan understand. I haven't suffered an allergy attack since I left Earth. The only thing I'm allergic to is cats." He sneezed again. "Let's go, Patty. Bye."

Molly giggled as Ralph fled through the door with Patty on his arm. Anna spun around and looked at where Molly was pointing. Suki sat on the dinette, calmly grooming herself.

Anna burst into giggles. She could still hear Ralph sneezing. Anna picked up the ragdoll cat who immediately went limp and started purring. Anna stroked the cat's rabbity fur. Suki smelled faintly of mint.

"Oh Suki, you stowaway! I'm so glad to see you. How did you do it? You fat thing. It's no wonder my luggage was overweight, but you weren't in there, were you? Molly did you hide Suki in the luggage?"

Molly gazed at her from with innocent eyes. "No Mama. Suki hides herself."

Anna stared at the cat, puzzled. "Well, we'll keep Suki hidden, somehow. Patty was chattering about rationing but they let you buy plenty to eat. We'll share with Suki."

Molly giggled and pointed at the floor. Anna frowned. The remains of a huge rat lay on the rug.

"Maybe she'll just feed herself." Anna made a face as she deposed of the remains. Suki floated lazily to the floor.

* * *

The next day Anna carefully locked Suki in the apartment, dropped Molly off at the daycare center and reported to hydrophonics.

The smell of mint and other plants refreshed her after the stale, hospital-smelling air of Luna City.

Her boss, Dr. Schneider, a bald, portly man of sixty or so, introduced her to her co-workers. Most were men who unconsciously straightened in Anna's presence.

She sighed. She didn't feel like dating. Brad had only been gone a year. She felt empty and alone but nobody could take his place. She became aware her attention had drifted and that Dr. Schenider was tapping the back of a young man who was working with an ailing plant.

Anna straightened and held out her hand, determined not to let this one stroke her hand or try any other suggestive behavior. He turned around and Anna found herself sinking into the deepest aqua eyes she had ever seen. Thick, tousled brown hair, boyish features, broad shoulders...perhaps Anna might have to change her mind about dating. To her surprise Dr. McLeod blushed as he took her hand, then instantly dropped it.

Dr. Schneider cleared his throat, looking amused. "You'll have to excuse Daniel. He's the shy type. I think if Luna City allowed cats, he would have a dozen cats and no dates. You'll be working closely with Dr. McLeod until you get the hang of things."

Anna smiled. "No problem. I love cats myself."

Daniel stared at his magnetos, his cheeks still flushed.

Anna smiled. So he was shy, that was sweet. Then she smothered a gasp. Was that Suki peeking out from behind his boots? She looked again. Nothing. Her heart slowed to its normal rate. No. Suki was safely locked in the apartment. A piece of stray cat hair lingered near the floor. Anna frowned. How did that get here? She checked the seat of her pants. No cat hair.

She saw Daniel watching her and blushed.

* * *

Anna's heart felt as light as her feet without her magneto's as she stopped to pick up Molly.

Ms. Daisy Stillwell smiled at them both as Anna hugged her daughter.

"My, that was a lovely toy your daughter had with her. I hope you know where she put it."

"Toy?"

"That cat toy covered with rabbit fur. Where is it now, Molly?"

Anna gulped, looking helplessly at her daughter. Just for a moment she thought she saw a cat, hovering over the hamster cage. Anna blinked, unable to believe her eyes. Nothing was there.

Molly giggled. "Suki just went home."

Ms. Stillwell shook her head. "Children and their imaginations. I hope you find it. My vision isn't what it used to be. I'm one hundred five years old, after all. I came to Luna City for my health. Wonderful low gravity. See you tomorrow."

Anna wondered a little about Ms. Stillwell's vision when she had several active childen to watch, but she came highly recomended. She and Molly hiked home as fast as she could in the unfamiliar magnetos. Molly had already adapted to them, so Anna had trouble keeping up with her daughter.

Anna nearly dropped her key in her hurry to unlock the apartment. It smelled wonderfully of mint. Didn't Daniel say something about growing mint and catnip in his office? Where else had she smelled mint today?

"Suki!"

"Meow."

Suki rested in the air with the remains of another rat. The cat had certainly adapted to the moon. Molly took off her magnetos and pushed up to pet the cat.

Anna discarded what was left of the rat. Nuisances. She'd found signs of rats in the apartment last night but obviously Suki was vanquishing them. Anna poured the cat a bowl of canned milk. Suki purred.

Anna sniffed. Suki smelled strongly of mint, peppermint. Peppermint plants had freshened the air at the preschool.

"Molly, did you bring Suki to school today? Did you take her home?"

Molly laughed, hugging the cat. "No Mama. She does it."

Anna turned and stared at the fluffy cat. Suki had finished her milk. Molly let her go and she purred and kneaded the air with her paws as she suddenly floated three feet above the carpet. She had to weigh something but she swam through the air like it was water.

How did that cat possibly get around without anyone seeing her? Especially out of a locked apartment. She had to be some kind of Houdini. At least she was smart enough to stay hidden from most adults. Fortunately, most adults tended to dismiss children's fanciful tales, in the event that any of Molly's classmates decided to share a story of a mysterious white kitty. The door pager beeped. "Molly, get Suki out of sight!"

Anna sighed and answered the door. "Please don't let it be Ralph," she said to nobody in particular.

Patty stood in the door way.

"Hi, Anna. It's me. Guess what! I set you up with Ralph's brother. We'll do a double date tonight. Don't worry about Molly. Old Mrs. Peterson wants to babysit."

"Please Patty. I haven't a thing to wear and I'm not dating."

"Oh, nonsense. You are too young and pretty to keep brooding about your late, late, late husband. Come on, live a little. We're going to the best restaurant on the moon."

Anna considered for a moment. What could it really hurt? "Oh, all right," she gave in.

An hour later Anna pushed George's hand off her knee under the table. She leaned away, evading his alcohol-ridden breath.

"Anna baby, you are a beauty. Do you put out on the first date?" he laughed. "Just kidding, baby."
Anna pushed his arm firmly away from her shoulders. "You're drunk, George."

He looked disappointed. "You know what's good about Luna City, baby? No babes with cats. Too many women on Earth were hung up on cats. Ralph and I hate them; the mangy, flea-bitten things give us allergies."

Anna smothered a laugh as she felt a warm, purring weight settle in her lap. A peppermint fragrance drifted to her nose.

George sneezed. Ralph followed, sneezing and coughing. Patty looked bewildered while Anna held back her giggles. Anna cleared her throat.

"I think it's time to call it a night. My little girl is probably getting restless."

George and Ralph beat a hasty retreat as Patty tried to hand Ralph an allergy spray.

Anna gave Suki a caress, feeling the cat purr. "Good girl, now go home, Suki."

* * *

Anna sighed as she stole a glance at Daniel Mcleod. Here was a man who liked cats. He stared at a crushed mint plant on his desk, muttering. "How in the world did this happen?"

"Dr. McLeod—I mean, Daniel. I see you have a calendar with cats on it. I've a ragdoll cat back home."

Daniel's face lit up with a smile that took Anna's breath away. "I love cats," he said. "I'm trying to convince the mayor to import cats to solve the rat problem but she keeps muttering about the cost. I've told her it will pay off immensely. Speaking of rats, there goes one. Look at him fly!"

The rat launched itself into the air like a flying squirrel. The next moment it was in the mouth of a larger flying object.

Anna gasped. "Suki. You followed me!" One moment the cat was not there, the next moment it was. Suki purred around the rat and disappeared. Both Daniel and Anna stared.

"A teleporting cat! Is she yours?"

"It's more like I'm hers. Suki, Suki, come here you bad girl!"

"I would say she's a good girl and this proves my point about cats and rats."

Anna laughed, the word rat bring a picture of George to mind. "Well, she certainly rescued me from a rat of a date last night."

Daniel stared at her, apparently surprised. "You've started dating again? I thought you were still grieving over your late husband."

"I guess I've recovered a lot since I left Earth. The change of scenery has helped immensely." She smiled. "Anyway, I need to figure out how keep Suki here legally."

Daniel shrugged and shuffled his feet. "Maybe we should talk it over in private, after work. Say dinner?"

"I'd love to! You say you know the mayor?"

Daniel smiled and nodded.

Her heart pounding, Anna smiled back at him, then went to check on her research. Time seemed to drag until quitting time. Daniel was waiting for her when she finished her work.

When Daniel walked Anna to her flat, they met George in the corridor outside her apartment.

"Hell-o Anna, gorgeous. I've been waiting for you to come home." He eyed Daniel. "I didn't know you had a boyfriend."

Daniel stopped and looked directly at the man. "Well now you know," he said softly.

Anna felt a flush of pleasure on her face.

"Uh, sorry," George muttered. "I'll see you around."

Anna nodded as she unlocked the door to her flat. Molly was staying at school an extra hour for "flying lessons." She and Daniel were finally alone; except for the plaintive meowing from her bedroom. They ditched their magnetos and Anna hurried to see what was wrong with Suki. She gasped at what she saw. "Kittens!"

Seven newborn kittens lay mewing in the middle of the bed. Daniel chuckled. "Some people are going to have a fit. Let's hope they have their mother's teleporting, telekinetic abilities."

"She *would* have them right in the middle of my bed!"

A tentative arm slipped about her waist. "There's always the couch?"

Anna laughed nervously, but then Daniel kissed her and they both floated off the floor, the cats forgotten.

* * *

A month later Suki's fate still hung in limbo.

Daniel and Anna were at work checking the plants when Dr. Schneider came to see how things were doing.

"The rat problem seems to be dwindling," he said, glancing around the perimeter of the room where the pests usually lingered, waiting for anything edible to drop within reach. "What are you using to kill them?"

Daniel cleared his throat cautiously as he glanced from Anna to their boss. "I've always said the best thing to kill a rat is a ..." Suki appeared in midair clutching a huge rat.

"...cat," Daniel finished weakly.

"How did that cat get on the moon?!" Dr. Snchneider blustered. "And how did it just appear out of the air like that?" He pointed at Suki. "It's breathing our air, drinking our water, eating our food and WHAT is it using for cat litter?"

Anna cleared her throat. "Suki stowed away on the rocket, Dr. Schneider, she began meekly. "She's my cat. I think she teleports herself somehow." Now Anna raised her chin defensively. "Mostly, she feeds herself. She uses shredded document paper for litter and she's no trouble at all. I'm sure whatever air she uses is more than made up for by the rats she kills before they can destroy the plants. Then nobody would be able to breathe."

"Possibly..." Dr. Schneider looked thoughtful. " It might warrant a bit more research. I'll make sure the cat is granted permission to stay—on probation, of course."

"I think the teleporting needs to remain a secret, sir," Daniel said firmly.

Dr. Schneider nodded.

Anna exchanged a relieve glance with Daniel. Nobody knew about the kittens yet, except Molly, and Anna had explained the importance of keeping the secret. Molly understood that they could lose the kittens if anybody knew about them.

Thankfully Anna, Daniel, Molly and the cats had been able to move in together into a bigger apartment. Bigger families were allowed more space and moving away from nosy Patty was imperative to keeping Suki and her family a secret.

That night dinner was interrupted by Molly's shriek. Anna and Daniel rushed into her bedroom and stopped in their tracks. Suki had a strange object in her mouth. As she dropped it, Daniel grabbed a pillowcase and used it to handle the thing.

"What is that?" Anna asked.

He examined it. "I don't know. I've never seen one before. It looks almost like a mouse-sized armadillo with six legs. Perhaps...it's a moon mouse?".

"But where did she get such a thing? We've found no life on the moon."

"I don't know. It could be a cave dweller. Look, it has tiny eyes and huge ears. Hmm... Since it's already dead, I'll take it to the lab for the guys to dissect."

* * *

On Saturday afternoon Anna came back from a meeting and found Daniel practically floating around the apartment.

"Our scientist conferred with the experts on Earth and

Suki's catch is a lunar animal! If she'd only show us where she found it, I'm sure we could get approval for the kittens," Daniel told Anna.

"Daniel, where is Molly?' she asked, looking around the flat.

"She was here just a minute ago. I think she said something about a new friend."

"Oh, no. I told her not to leave the apartment by herself. I asked you to keep an eye on her!" Anna felt panic and anger grip her by the throat.

Daniel flushed. "I didn't know a kid could vanish so fast. I just went to get her lunch."

A sudden rumbling shook the building and continued to grow stronger. Anna turned pale. "Moonquake!" she gasped. "Daniel, we have to find Molly, now!"

Daniel caught her by the shoulders. "No, wait until it stops. Suki will find Molly. Trust me."

Anna clung to Daniel as the ground shook and they both floated into the air. Anna sobbed. *Where was Molly? Where was her baby?* Finally, the shaking subsided, leaving cups and plates floating gently about the room, which eventually came to rest on the floor.

"Suki," Daniel called, "find Molly." Suki meowed, then vanished, reappeared, and meowed again. The cat moved to the door and they followed her out.

Anna breathed a sigh of relief as she gazed at the sky. "At least the dome didn't crack."

Anna followed Suki anxiously, Daniel one step behind her. "Oh, no!" Anna gasped when she saw that Suki was headed for the Lunar museum. The quake had damaged it quite heavily, and if Molly was inside...

Daniel and Anna followed Suki to a dark corner of the

museum where a large crack had appeared in the floor and cold air came rushing from it.

"Meow!" Suki disappeared.

"MOLLY!" Anna cried. "If anything's happened to her, I'll never forgive you, Daniel McLeod."

Suki reappeared and butted Daniel's hands. He stuck his head in the three and a half foot diameter hole and shouted. "Molly! Molly, swim back up here, baby!"

A faint cry came to them. "I can't. I'm stuck."

"Keep her talking, Anna!" Daniel got to his feet and sprinted away, disappearing around a corner. Anna stared atfter him. *Where was he going? How could he leave them like this?* Suki vanished and Anna heard Molly calling.

"Mama, Suki's here."

"We'll get you both out, just hang on, baby."

A panting Daniel reappeared at her elbow with a rope and a hard hat mounted with a light, where he'd gotten them, she didn't know. He tied the rope about his waist and handed it to the gathering crowd of spectators that had followed close on Daniel's heels. Stripping off his magnetos he climbed head-first down the hole. Camera newsmen shoved their way to the front of the crowd,.

The first thing to come floating out the hole was Suki.

"A cat!" the crowd roared. Then Molly came floating out of the hole into Anna's outstetched arms. Daniel followed, his face awestricken.

"There is an entire network of ice caves down there. Huge caverns of water and oxygen—in the form of ice. That must be where Suki found the moon mouse."

* * *

Anna and Daniel sat on the couch listening to the news but watching Molly and Suki play with the kittens. Then one story caught their attention.

"The ragdoll cats are now official citizens of the moon and Suki, the mother cat, was given the key to Luna City. Officials say life on the moon is getting easier with sources of air and water from previously undiscovered subsurface ice stores. News correspondent Bob Smith is at the scene. Bob, what can you tell us about how these ice stores are being used."

"Well Fran, Luna City is using the caves in several ways. The primary use is for water and oxygen as you mentioned, but the discovery also opens the doors for a more entertaining purpose. The Jaxco Lunar Company is developing a huge flying cave with a luxury hotel as it's anchor attraction. Wealthy Earth citizens are already signing waiting lists for the first visit. As reward for discovering the caves, Daniel and Anna McLeod have been given the best suites in the hotel. Looks like soon everyone will be moving underground. I'm Bob Smith, reporting live. Back to you."

Anna sighed and glanced at the diamond ring on her finger. In addition to the hotel suite, there had also been a monetary bonus for eradicating the rats. All together it had paid for a very nice wedding, and they would be moving into the hotel as soon as it was finished.

Suki's teleporting kittens were sold and a ragdoll mate would soon be here to join Suki. A scent of peppermint drifted to Anna and she glanced over at Suki. The cat purred, then blinked out of sight.

"I wonder where she goes these days to catch all those moon mice," Anna remarked idly.

A moment later, Suki returned, in the arms of a small being with three eyes in a wedge-shaped head. It whistled something like, "uh oh." The humans froze in shock as the small saurian biped stared back and cleared its throat.

"I suppose the correct terminology would be—take me to your leader."

About the Author:

Ellen Dawn Benefield has had stories published in Computer Edge, Millennium science fiction and Fantasy Magazine, Bardic Runes and various other magazines. She is a member of SFWA and is currently working on a science fiction novel and polishing three fantasy novels. She is an eclectic individual who has trained horses, bred Shelties, taught riding and dancing, including ethnic and belly dancing, and of course, she has four cats.

ellenbenefield@echelonpress.com

Dreams, Screams, and Lending Schemes

Linda DeMeulemeester

Dreams, Screams, and Lending Schemes

That night there had been no hint in the chill night air of the strange turn our fates would take. Sally was only soup and salad then. I wasn't even an appetizer.

Sally parked her minivan outside my house and had honked. "Roz, we can't be late." Her voice pierced my double glazed windows.

"I'm heading out now," I told my family as I jammed the last plate into the dishwasher.

"What do you mean, Mom?" James, my thirteen-year-old deepened his voice accusingly. "You were supposed to help me with my homework."

"Sorry. What is it you wanted me to do?" I glanced out the window and waved for Sally to hang on. Then I looked at the back of Brian's head hoping he'd intervene. No such luck, my husband was glued to the hockey game as usual.

"I need you to type my book report." James hauled the novel, *War of the Worlds*, and a huge wad of paper out of his backpack and handed them to me.

"I can type it up when I get home." I tossed the work on the hall desk and grabbed my jacket and purse.

"There won't be enough time. You need to write some of it for me too." James' freckles puckered around his frown.

I sighed. "When's it due?"

"Tomorrow." Panic edged his voice up a notch.

"Well, if we get up really early..."

"But I need you to help me finish the book," he whined.

"Look, I passed grade eight." I passed him book, then walked out the door.

"You never get as good marks as the other mothers anyhow."

Sally waved. "C'mon Roz, hurry."

"Mom! My shirt—it shrank. You ruined it!" Sarah, my sixteen-year-old daughter, stormed onto the porch in a red-faced fury.

James joined her shouting, "Mom." I heard my husband turn up the volume of the television to filter out all the background noise.

I rushed toward the van.

"My life is ruined!"

"Mom. Mom!"

I slammed the door. A flying saucer must have replaced my beautiful little girl with an alien pod. And then it returned for my son. I decided acne was the harbinger of these changelings.

Sally shot out of the driveway. I sank exhausted into my seat and mumbled, "I'm not sure about this. Explain it to me again."

"It's called *micro-credit*. It's about women helping women." Sally wove her van along the highway. "And when I'm gifted, I'll front you the thousand dollars to join, like Lisa did for me, and her friend did for her. I'm soup and salad now."

I'd read about micro-credit and how it had made a huge impact on the poorest women in third world countries. A group of women would receive a loan, and it would go to one woman. She'd use the money to start a business, and when her business succeeded she would pay the loan back, and another woman would borrow the money. They all had an invested interest in helping each other, so the money could be passed to the next woman. It was enormously successful. I'd even seen a television special on how micro-credit had started in up the Pacific Northwest, where some women operated a llama farm. But...

"Nobody's doing anything for the money except joining up. And why is it so secretive. Something's not right. That's not micro-credit, it's a..."

"Listen," Sally said. "Roscas have worked in Nairobi for hundreds, maybe thousands of years. Women in the village throw money in the pot. Each woman gets a turn keeping it. This is the same idea—a lending circle. It's my turn you know." Sally's voice caught. "Here's my chance."

I held my tongue because I wanted to believe for Sally. She was a single mom. Her two grown sons still lived at home. She'd worked extra shifts to pay the bills and asked them for nothing, hoping they'd save their own money for college. But the oldest son had come back after his first term with his pregnant girlfriend in tow. Sally was now supporting Mom, Dad and junior. As for her second son, his money always went into, well, recreational stuff that people got arrested for.

"You'll see at the meeting. It really changes women's lives." Sally parked in front of a pastel suburban home with all the trimmings: trellises, flocked lace curtains, hardly a den for illegal activities. Several women in leisurewear, Nikes and blow-dried hair emerged from their cars and fell in sync toward the door. I brushed back the graying strands of my own disheveled hair and tucked my shirt inside my jeans. I wished I'd showered first, put on make up, something.

"It looks like a Tupperware party." I joked, though butterflies collapsed, collected, and formed a solid lump in my stomach. Something wasn't right; the way those women uniformly streamed in felt creepy. But Sally sported a new hairdo, red streaks and all. She looked fresher and younger than she had in years. I followed her inside the house.

The living room had that Martha Stewart touch. Ladies grouped around chair settings sipping Darjeeling tea and nibbling from plates of olive pinwheel and salmon ribbon sandwiches. I looked around hoping to see wineglasses set out. They weren't.

"Which ones are rich now?" I elbowed Sally.

"Shh, Roz. It's never announced. You know, for tax n' stuff. Flashing your money isn't encouraged."

"Then," I spun around taking in all the eager whispers and hopeful faces, "then," this time I whispered too. "How do you know this isn't a hoax, and nobody's made any money?"

"Oh, you know." Sally forgot she'd been whispering. "Those women positively shine. You can actually see them glow."

I perused the group for 'glow in the dark' women until I noticed some of the small talk had stopped and our conversation was being observed. The kitchen door opened and a shadow darted behind it. The hostess, who I thought looked a little shiny, got up from a wing-backed chair, scurried to the kitchen, and disappeared behind the door. When she emerged she called Sally over. I squirmed, uncomfortable in my seat. Just like at parent association meetings, I never quite fit in. I watched them chat until the hostess smiled and patted Sally on the shoulder.

"Well?" I asked when Sally sat back on the loveseat beside me. "Are they kicking me out for being suspicious and not buying into this?"

"No," Sally smiled. "They always have to be cautious; you know, not let the patriarchy infiltrate the group."

I wondered when she said patriarchy if she had meant police.

Sally touched my hand. "Don't worry. I told Lisa you were skeptical, but you were really a sister in need."

"Sister in need," I laughed. "What's that supposed to mean?" But Sally didn't elaborate and as the evening progressed and I heard testimonials from the rest of the women, I began thinking how cash might make a difference in my life. The final gift was $50,000, and you could reenter on the bottom any time you liked, so most women never left the lending group. I squashed my suspicions. With some of that money I could change my research assistant job to part-time, and build that sunroom off the kitchen I'd always dreamed of, the one Brian would never agree to. I could say I won a contest. My own little spot, somewhere to sip my tea, or on some nights a stiff scotch, maybe eat a few chocolates, read my novels. Yes, I'd line one wall with bookshelves and stack it with hardcover books, never wait for the paperback versions. And when the kids got too demanding, or I got tired of Brian ignoring me, I could slip in there and shut the door. Escape.

I wondered when I had changed—when books were good enough. That wasn't the Roz Welles in my year-book; the person voted most likely to climb Mount Everest. Maybe it was time to take a risk. I began paying closer attention to what was required of me if I joined up.

After the meeting, Sally and I didn't drive off immediately. Instead, we sat in the van and fine-tuned our plans. The lending group levels progressed from appetizer, to soup and salad, entree, then finished with dessert. Next week I'd be fronted $5000 and enter as an appetizer, and that would bump Sally up to entree. Then it was just a matter of time until we'd be gifted. All I had to do was bring in someone new.

"The problem is, I don't have many friends."

"That's okay," said Sally. "Bring someone in who could bring another woman in right away. Then that person will be an appetizer and fronted $5000 dollars. And you'll be bumped up faster, where the big money is. You don't have to know a lot of women. Just choose the right woman, someone who could initiate others quickly.

"Darcie," we both said at once. I let myself feel excited. It hadn't occurred to me yet that at no point did I have to spend a single dollar. I was too busy scheming. "What will you do with your money?"

Sally's face relaxed and got that dreamy look. I was expecting her to say something about straightening out her sons, setting things on track.

"I could afford my own grocery boy."

Grocery boy was Sally's term for all those young, handsome looking men, the type that worked at the supermarket; the ones that always looked so eager to please you. That's what I liked about Sally. She looked like an earnest hard working mother on the outside, but underneath she could take my mind where my Catholic body wasn't allowed to go.

Sally started the van. Before we turned the corner, we saw the hostess drive by in a black, outdated Chevy Nova. The man beside her wore a black fedora and black overcoat and wraparound sunglasses.

"If your friend Lisa's been gifted, she's sure not using the money to buy a new car or update her husband's wardrobe," I pointed out.

"That's not her husband."

"Oh,' was all I could think to say.

The next afternoon I met Darcie in the restaurant of her fitness club. When I arrived, Darcie was waiting at the table.

The wear and tear of middle years did not rest upon Darcie's lightly tanned brow. Her gold streaked hair fell in thick tresses past her shoulders. Her make-up looked professional. Her slim athletic figure flattered the tightly belted, short- skirted suit. And high heels. She always wore high heels. I inhaled, sucking in my stomach as I walked to our table and gratefully released my breath when I sat down.

I stared at the menu. I could stick to the fat busters diet if I ordered the brown rice casserole. The steak and salad would fit into a low carbohydrate plan, but I was sick of that one. I decided on the veggie burger, vegetarians were always thin. I asked for a side of fries – potatoes were vegetables. Darcie chose a garden salad with dressing on the side. When we ordered Spanish Coffees, Darcie asked for no sugar on the rim of her glass. It occurred to me that being a trophy wife carried a price.

"So," I asked after filling her in on my clandestine adventures. "Are you interested?"

"Oh, count me in." Darcie stabbed her fork into her salad.

"I have to tell you, Sally says this is micro-credit, a women's lending circle. But no one invests in a business and then pays others back. It's a matter of making more money as more people join under you." I frowned, wondering at my willingness to believe the night before. "It's a pyramid scheme, I think. And everything's so secret."

"Are women making money?" Darcie tapped a French-polished nail on the table.

"I think so, but..."

"Forget the details then. Menages are women's credit circles in Scotland. They've been going on for hundreds of years. They're secret so women can keep the money, and the men can't take it." Darcie crunched a celery stick.

Darcie, too - how come everyone knew about this stuff but me? I had the college degree. She missed a point though. "Can you get arrested for joining a rosca or a menage like you can for belonging to a pyramid?" I inhaled the inviting steam of my French fries.

"Look, the stock market is about buying low and selling high. That's a money scheme." Darcie pounded the table. "The only difference is that men built Wall Street. They wrote the laws, and they didn't include the same principal of economy for the female psyche. This is more than investment and capital. It's friends helping friends. Screw the criminal code."

Never had anything made so much sense. But Darcie had plenty of money. I was curious and asked, "What's in it for you?"

Darcie pursed her collagen lips. "Either I become very independent while helping other women, or I'm arrested and I get to see on the news how the wife of a prominent judge is involved in a pyramid scheme. It's a win - win situation."

My throat tightened. Why had I envied her? "Do you think you'll be able to recruit anyone new?"

She laughed. "Every woman in my gym for a start."

I reveled in the momentary bliss and was about to bite into my veggie burger when my cell phone rang. Darcie arched her eyebrow.

"Mom," Sarah screeched in my ear. "I've broken my skirt zipper and I have to walk around in my coat. You have to pick me up from school now."

"Give me thirty minutes, Sarah. I've just started my lunch." I watched Darcie keep a poker face. She had opinions about my parenting, but not being a mother herself, she never offered advice. I liked her for that.

"Mom. Now."

"Twenty minutes," I bargained.

"I hate you." My cell phone went dead. Sighing I slipped it back in my purse. I lifted up my burger but my cell went off again. "What?" I sighed.

"Roz Welles? This is James' principal. He's had an accident skateboarding in the school cafeteria. He's having his arm set in a cast at emergency now. We'll talk about his suspension later."

"I'll be right there. Have you contacted my husband?"

The principal cleared his throat. "Um, yes, he asked if you could pick up his dry cleaning on the way back from the hospital."

I stood up at the table.

"Don't leave your French fries in front of me," was all Darcie said.

Sarah pouted in the back of my van while James complained. "If you had bought me the good skate boarding equipment, this wouldn't have happened."

We pulled into our driveway while I dreamed of a little vacation somewhere on my own. Maybe that would be possible now.

* * *

Everything fell into place, and it wasn't a week before Sally was dessert and I was an entree. Darcie and I had arrived at Sally's house together. Sally was hosting her first investment group meeting. Her modest rental looked spruced with new deck chairs on the porch, and hanging baskets. Money must have fallen her way. There were several cash prizes that would appear when you became dessert. Sometimes money arrived in a hollowed out cookbook left on your porch. Or a bag of groceries would be delivered with cookie boxes stuffed with cash. It was only a taste, though, of the big cash prize. When you actually became gifted, it was rumored to involve an exclusive ceremony and dinner at an expensive retreat.

We flocked through the door with the other women; a low whistle escaped Darcie. New curtains, new carpet, new couch, Sally was doing all right. When she came out of the kitchen carrying a tray of lemon squares and butter tarts, it was my turn to whistle. Sally didn't glow—she was luminous. I began to wonder if she'd already been gifted.

"Hey Sally," I teased. "Looks like you can afford to forget the tea and break out the champagne." Sally ignored my remark. Several women gave me that look some people are so good at, that one of mild disapproval. I didn't get any champagne.

Throughout the evening I tried approaching Sally. How much money did she get? But it was impossible. She just glided in and out of her kitchen, nodding and smiling. I could elicit only brisk comments from her. Shiny Sally didn't seem herself.

"What's with her?" Darcie confirmed.

I shrugged. At the end of the evening, Darcie and I hung back as the last of the women filtered out. We tidied crumbs, picked up teacups, and headed for the kitchen. Sally blocked our entrance and through smiling lips told us she could manage. She grabbed our trays, opened the kitchen door a crack and laid them on the table. Then with surprising firmness she grasped our elbows and guided us out the front door.

"Sally," I grabbed the door jam, resisting. "I just want to know how you're doing."

"Everything is wonderful," she said in a monotone voice. She gave me what I thought was going to be a gentle shove, but it launched me out onto the porch, and then she closed the door. I rubbed my elbow. When did she get so strong?

"What was that about?" Darcie checked the driveway. There was only one car besides ours left—a black Chevy Nova. Darcie observed me rubbing my shoulder. "Strange."

We walked back to my car and climbed in. I drove up the block and then circled back past the house on a hunch. Darcie and I saw 'glow in the dark' Sally, pull out in the Chevy Nova. The man at the wheel wore a black fedora, black overcoat and wraparound sunglasses.

"Strange," Darcie said again.

I tried to call Sally five or six times during that week. I only got her answering machine. Darcie drove by her house. She saw number one son, wife and child sporting a minivan, and number two son leaving the house with a new snowboard and stepping into a sharp looking recreation vehicle, but no Sally.

Meanwhile, I ascended the levels of our lending group, thanks to the endless stream of women Darcie recruited from her gym. I was dessert now, and I had found on two occasions a box of cake mix left at my doorstep. Both the packages were stuffed with fifty-dollar bills. With that money I'd bought precooked gourmet meals for Brian, new skateboard equipment and Cole's notes for James, and new clothes for Sarah. My family didn't notice I was hardly there anymore.

One night, after another meeting and another failed attempt to penetrate Sally's plastic persona, Darcie and I left the pyramid meeting early. Tea and scones didn't cut it. We stopped at a bar and ordered a drink.

"It's not just Sally," Darcie said after she less than daintily chugged her gin fizz. "I can't get through to Lisa either."

I shrugged my shoulders. "I don't know Lisa very well."

"I don't either, but think. You've met her several times. What was she like?"

It was funny. I hadn't noticed before, but, well, "I thought Sally could be a little raunchy. Lisa sputtered expletives like a storm trooper."

"And now," Darcie prompted.

"Flat as three day old ginger ale." It was an epiphany.

"It's not only Sally and Lisa. I've been making the rounds at these meetings."

Darcie was good at that, small talk and chatter.

"About a quarter of the women utter the same phrases all the time."

Sally, too. She attended all the meetings, but our conversations reminded me of those new computerized dolls they have on the market. The toys' responses are uncanny in their appropriateness to the situation, but they use a limited number of stock phrases.

"What do you think, Darcie?" I was at a loss. "When they get their final gift," I stumbled. "If Sally went to the retreat for her celebration, did she become indoctrinated into a cult?"

She shook her head. "Cults take time. Sally changed over night." Darcie frowned thoughtfully. "I once read in the National Exposure about strange herbs that turn people into zombies. It makes them susceptible to mental programming."

And to think I disdained Darcie's penchant for tabloid news. I remembered the peculiar smell of all the tea they served at the meetings, but decided it was only the unfamiliar scent of an expensive brand. Still, what did women drink and eat at the gifting retreat? And besides...

"Why program these women, load them up with money and let them loose?"

"We have to find out," Darcie said in a breathless rush. "For Sally's sake."

* * *

I turned over for the hundredth time on my bed that night. I hadn't really believed Sally was a victim of illicit programming. But something was wrong. I turned to Brian; he was a police sergeant after all. He'd turned off the late news and was lying on his side.

"I've got a problem," I said softly. I charged ahead before I changed my mind. "I've sort of stumbled into a..." There was no way around it. I was guilty, guilty of getting involved in a pyramid scheme, guilty of sins of omission, guilty. I spilled my story.

Brian was silent. I squirmed and waited for his input. The only input he gave, however, was a loud snore. I suddenly realized that Darcie and I were in this alone.

The next day a box of chocolates arrived at my door. I opened it. Underneath the first layer were rolls of one hundred-dollar bills, and a note. It said,

> *Prepare to be gifted. Tonight please join us at Grover's Mill Retreat (no guests). We are located off highway 101, at the junction of Chilliwack and Harrison Lake exit. Drive up the logging road, three kilometers to the retreat.*

I didn't touch the chocolates in case they had a touch of zombie ingredients. I called Darcie right away. "This is it," I said. "Meet me at the junction of the highway."

Darcie's calm demeanor impressed me.

"Don't be ten seconds late," her voice rasped.

Okay, maybe not that calm.

Part of me realized I only half believed everything that had happened over these last few weeks. I was an ordinary person. Yet, I went behind my husband's back, joined an illegal pyramid, raked easy money in, and became a bystander as my best friend underwent a mysterious transformation. And now I'd convinced myself to drive up to Grover's Mill Retreat.

I pulled off the highway. Darcie was waiting for me. I couldn't decide if I was relieved or terrified. She backed her car into a small clearing off the highway. I opened up the passenger door.

"I'm supposed to go alone. You'd better hide now. Who knows, they might have look-outs or binoculars."

"They?" Darcie crouched below the dashboard.

I rattled off instructions. I was impressed with myself, though not necessarily reassured. "Let me go in first. If we bring the authorities in now, we won't find out how they transform these women."

"How long should I wait for you?"

I'd never seen anyone outside the investment group but that one man in the not too trendy black outfit. And no woman had gone missing or looked frightened or hurt. "If I'm not out in twenty minutes get help."

Darcie tried nodding, but it was hard all crunched down like that under the dash.

I pulled into a long, meandering driveway at the front of the sprawling retreat. With the exception of us, the rest of the place appeared morgue quiet. I felt each and every goose bump erupt on my flesh. I opened the car door before I could panic and run.

"Roz," Darcie stage whispered to me through her clenched teeth. "Twenty minutes."

A person couldn't become zombified in twenty minutes. I lifted the heavy knocker on the huge oak door and banged it down twice. It then occurred to me that way up here on a logging road it could still take police an hour before they arrived. Sweat prickled my forehead. A quiet gloom set in as the day edged toward twilight. The door opened.

No light escaped from behind the oak door. I couldn't make out the emerging silhouette. I didn't know whom I was expecting, but it wasn't...

"Sally?"

"Hi, Roz." Sally leaned past me and nodded toward my car. "Tell Darcie to come on in." Sally wasn't exactly glowing this evening, but she looked thinner, and happy.

Darcie climbed the steps casting suspicious glances between Sally and what waited behind the door, and then Sally disappeared behind it. I held back. Something wasn't right.

Darcie leaned toward me and whispered. "Don't worry, I have a back up plan."

We stepped over the threshold and into the retreat. Sally walked ahead of us down the dim hall and this time I whispered into Darcie's ear.

"We eat nothing. In case it's not the food, but some kind of indoctrination, how's your sales resistance?"

"Not so good." She sounded rueful. "I'm here in this mess with you, aren't I? And in case there's trouble, I hit high - you hit low."

I stopped, incredulous. "That was your plan?" We were doomed. Sally paused at the end of the long hall and waited for us to catch up. We entered a small, rustic parlor with the biggest stone fireplace I'd ever seen. In this light I noticed Sally did look a little shiny. Uneasiness crept up my spine. Before we had a chance to ask her what's been going on, a second door across the room opened up. That weird character I'd seen driving away with Lisa and later with Sally, walked in. I heard another noise and spun around. A second man in black walked through the first door. We were cut off.

"Men in Black. They're men in black!" Darcie shouted.

"I can see that," I said stupidly.

"No," Darcie rushed toward the door. "I mean, they're aliens."

Now I understood. I didn't read Darcie's tabloids, but I read science fiction. We were about to be the victims of an alien abduction. I ran too. When the second guy blocked the doorway, Darcie and I fell into plan 'B'. I noticed how all that time Darcie spent at her gym paid off. When Darcie hit high, the guy went flying.

"C'mon, Sally," we shouted, but two arms grabbed me and tugged me back into the room. One of the arms was Sally's; the other was the first man in black. Meanwhile, the second guy recovered and was struggling with Darcie.

"Stop." Sally gasped. "They're not 'men in black,' they're—"

In my struggles I knocked the hat off the one that had been holding me, and I realized Sally was right. They weren't men in black.

"Women!" Darcie exclaimed.

I stared in surprise as long blonde hair tumbled down the shoulders of my aspiring captor.

"Actually we are travel agents." She patted back her disheveled hair.

"We don't want to abduct you. We work for Paradox Travels Incorporated, and are here on behalf of clients on an alternate world that would like to swap lives with you—not permanently mind you—for a few months at a time. And our clients are willing to pay a lot of money for that service."

Darcie slowed her struggle, but looked confused. The National Examiner probably didn't cover alternate universes.

"It's a lucrative business." The other woman in black took her hat off and shook out a mop of dark curly hair. They weren't so identical after all. I could see why they disguised themselves though; women would remember their looks. She undid the top button of her black overcoat and continued explaining.

"Women from a parallel universes want stress free vacations while experiencing a different culture. While there are millions of alternate worlds, this planet always shows up as the most optimal for our clients."

"What do you mean?" I felt a little insulted, but I wasn't sure why.

The brunette W.I.B. smiled hesitantly." On this Earth, the swap between you and your counterparts is always minimally disruptive."

Minimally disruptive - I recalled the plastic frozen smiles and the stock phrases from those other women at the meetings. "What happens when our families discover that a different Roz, Darcie and Sally from some other universe have replaced us?"

"Your parallel replacements will look exactly like you, except for a slight sheen they'll acquire when they pass through the Paradox Particle Accelerator." So that's why Sally was shiny.

"Also, we prep our clients in 'stock conversation procedures' and we keep the cash flowing, so..." This time she pulled at a brown strand of hair, and her voice hinted discomfort. "No one's ever found out," she finished.

The room fell silent. I remembered my own family never questioning how often I'd been gone lately, as long as meals were served and the treats kept coming. The two W.I.B.'s had let Darcie and me go, but neither of us moved. Sally waited.

"What's in it for us?" I asked.

Sally turned effervescent. "I'm telling you it's an amazing life. I've just returned from a parallel universe where dinosaurs never became extinct. Would you believe I'm a tour guide on that world? And now there's a Sally who wants me to take over in a universe where Mars kept its atmosphere, and there's an interplanetary coalition. That Sally's the captain of a space crew." She broke off dreamy eyed and looked up at me. "I've been back to meet her, I mean, my crew. On a scale of ten, if you rate grocery boys three, these men would be about a fifteen."

That was my friend sounding back to normal. I relaxed a bit. But...

I felt dizzy. "Who are the women they want Darcie and me to replace?"

"Whoever they are, it's going to be better than here," said Darcie. "My time with the pyramid has been the most exciting in my life, and that's before we're even bounced into some other universe."

"Who—where?" I insisted.

"A retired general of Amazon fighting troops is looking for a vacation. Your doppelganger is currently escorting tours up Mount Olympus on Mars. She climbs the highest mountain in the solar system." The blonde W.I.B. saw my look of astonishment.

"Don't worry, she said, "It's only one third gravity there."

She'd misread my expression. I remembered my yearbook notation, and my rappelling gear gathering dust in my attic. The shock I had felt was like finding a pair of high heel shoes and putting them on and feeling like I'd found shoe heaven. It fit.

"Well?" Sally asked.

I thought of my last few weeks. If those parallel universe women thought our lives were stress free, they'd be in for a surprise. Still, it made sense, what a different life they'd find here, a perfect guise for playing amateur anthropologists. I thought of my kids. Should I warn those women the natives were hostile? I'd wanted to build a sunroom where I could sit and read about adventure. Did I have the courage to try the real thing?

"What do you think?" Darcie asked this time. "I bet I'll replace someone important."

When Darcie said this the blonde W.I.B. smiled. "You'd be replacing an intergalactic economics professor."

Darcie beamed. "I knew it. I have some really good theories I can lecture on."

Could we pull it off? Sally had been doing fine. And those women from parallel universes were essentially us. I had to have it in me somewhere. Then I thought of my family and how Brian and the kids would make out when an Amazon general replaced me. "What the hell." I shrugged.

Darcie nodded in agreement. On cue, the wall behind the huge stone fireplace dilated and a metallic portal appeared. Sally, Darcie and I walked through it together, and I could hear a pulsating thrum. I could also hear the travel agents' voices behind me.

"We need to work on our recruitment strategies."

"Why? Every woman who enters our pyramid agrees to switch."

"Yes, but this time I think I got a broken rib."

About the Author:

Linda DeMeulemeester lives and works as an adult education instructor in British Columbia. A while ago her addiction to reading science fiction escalated to include writing it. After attending Clarion West Writers' Workshop, there was no going back. As far as she knows there are no twelve step programs for this, and self-help tapes didn't work. She has a short story soon to appear in the science fiction magazine, NeoOpsis.

Ish Kabibble's Books

Karen Duvall

Ish Kabibble's Books

"I won't be long, I promise," Margie told her husband. "Why don't you go find a bookstore, buy a newspaper or magazine to read while I shop?"

Dover rolled his eyes, silently wishing he were anywhere but here. "You know how much I hate shopping malls."

"I know, honey," his wife said, clutching Dover's arm and leading him to the mall directory. "But you need to get out into the world now and then. You're too young to work as much as you do. Remember: All work and no play..."

"Shopping is not my idea of 'play.'

Margie let go of him and crossed her arms over her ample breasts. She gave him that impatient look that always made him feel like a child. "It's the dinner and a movie afterward that I'm talking about."

"Oh." Dover felt too distracted to enjoy a movie. What he really wanted to do was go home and finish balancing the books for one of his firm's biggest clients. He'd barely made a dent in the ledger files and a full report was due Monday morning.

Margie made a show of checking her watch. She pointed at it and said, "Give me one hour. All I need is a pair of shoes and matching purse to go with the dress I bought last week."

Dover pinched the bridge of his nose and sighed. "Only an hour?"

His wife nodded and stepped back from the directory, squinting as she read over the list of stores. She pointed to a blue square on the map. "I'll be right here."

"Then I'll wait for you..." Dover turned in a circle and spotted a bench flanked by two potted palms. Behind it was a small fountain that spewed plumes of water in regular intervals. It looked like a pleasant enough spot. "I'll wait for you there."

His wife frowned. "Isn't there at least something you want to shop for? You could use a new pair of shoes, or how about that book on World War II you've been wanting to read?"

He shrugged. "I don't know. I'd rather just stay here." And take a nap, he thought. Maybe then he wouldn't fall asleep during the movie.

"No you wouldn't." She glanced at the directory again. "Look here. There's a Borders right upstairs from where we're standing."

Not wanting to argue, Dover said, "Fine." He headed for the escalator.

"Haven't you forgotten something?" Margie asked sweetly.

He planted a quick, dry kiss on her cheek.

She patted his face and grinned, her eyes dancing with the excitement of having a full hour to ogle shoes and purses at her favorite department store. "Have fun, Dover. And don't buy out the bookstore!" She blew him a kiss, then trotted off down the lane of brightly lit shops and neon store signs, her round little bottom bouncing with each click of her spike-heeled shoes.

Dover noticed several men turn their heads to watch her walk by. "I wish she wouldn't wear such tight jeans," he mumbled to himself. He felt a twinge of jealousy, but nothing strong enough to send him running after her. The torture of sharing her shopping experience was more than he was willing to suffer in the name of chivalry.

He started for the escalator, then paused. Did he really want to meander through the crowded, overstocked aisles of a mall bookstore? He gazed longingly at the bench by the waterfall, but he was too keyed up for a nap. Maybe he'd just wander around for an hour, check out one of those novelty stores that sold high tech gizmos like automatic dog washers and supersonic back scratchers. It was second best to a bookstore, but it would do.

For a Saturday afternoon, the mall wasn't nearly as crowded as he thought it would be. He passed an arcade, where a dozen teenagers hung around blinking machines that dinged and rattled with every point scored. The music pouring from the open doorway rumbled with a base so deep he could feel it through his shoes. Next door was a popcorn vendor called the *Snack Shack* that also sold soft pretzels. The aroma of popped corn and yeasty, hot pretzels made his mouth water, but he must save his appetite for his dinner with Margie.

Around the corner from the *Snack Shack* was a shallow alcove that held a luggage shop and an upscale jewelry store with barred display windows. Between them stood an interesting little retailer with a bedraggled sign that read *Ish Kabibble's Books.*

"Aha!" Dover said aloud. "Just the place I was looking for."

He approached the store eagerly, but slowed once he neared the storefront. The walls looked aged, as if made from that old barn wood that was so popular with decorators these days. The cobwebs shrouding the display window gave it an eerie authenticity; he wondered if this was a leftover from last week's Halloween decorations. The store itself could have come straight from a remote village street out of sixteenth century Europe. Dover was no historian, but he recognized the old English typeface used to print the yellowed posters mounted on the cloudy glass. "Adventures for the mind sold here," one of them said. "Experience the world without leaving home," said another.

He wondered what kinds of books were sold here. Travel books? He wasn't much of a traveler, the extent of his journeys taking him no farther than the Bahamas, where he and Margie had spent their honeymoon three years ago. Perhaps this wasn't the store for him after all. It looked closed anyway.

As Dover turned to leave, he heard the creak of stubborn hinges followed by the jingle of a bell. He looked over his shoulder, noticing the door was now ajar and that warm, yellow light shone through the narrow opening. An OPEN sign hung from the rusty door knob. He was certain the sign hadn't been there a moment ago.

He shrugged and walked into the shop.

"Can I help you find something in particular?" came a cheerful voice from behind him.

Dover spun around to see an elderly man behind an ancient-looking sales counter. His snowy hair was streaked with reddish strands that seemed to glow beneath the ceiling lights. His gray eyes twinkled, making him look like a slimmed down version of Santa Claus, except that Santa had pointed ears, not fleshy lobes that hung low enough to reach this man's shoulders. Several pieces of jewelry dangled from his elongated ears, including two wire loops, each one glistening with a half-dozen gold and silver charms.

Dover tried not to stare when he asked, "What kinds of books do you sell here?"

The shopkeeper gave his head a little shake, causing his myriad earrings to jangle almost as loud as the door's bell. "All kinds," he said. "You'll not see a selection like this anywhere else, I can assure you."

Clearly a con man, Dover thought. "Is that right?"

"Absolutely." The old man leaned forward and extended his right hand. "The name's Ish Kabibble. Pardon my manners for not standing. Rheumatism. Hits me hard during the rainy season."

Dover scowled while shaking the man's hand. "It's bone dry outside. Has been for weeks." Which was typical of the Arizona desert most of the time.

The old man sputtered, snatching up a pair of round eyeglasses and dropping them onto the bridge of his bulbous nose. The glasses had no lenses.

"Quite right, my boy," he said to Dover, while searching the counter for an illusive item he never did find. He stopped fidgeting and said, "I've been out of town, in a place where it rains a lot."

"I see." Dover studied the tidy store, impressed by the orderly arrangement of volumes stacked on the shelves. "So you're Ish Kabibble, the store's owner?"

"The one and only," Ish Kabibble said. "That is, if you don't count the 1930s comedian of the same name."

"You were named after him?"

"Actually, I chose the name myself. People had a hard time pronouncing my other one."

Though curious about the old man's former name, Dover only nodded and wandered down an aisle. He tugged a book from the shelf, its cover smooth and bright with a bluish-green gloss, patterns of spirals and octagons coating its surface. On close inspection it looked as if made from snake skin, though Dover had never heard of a snake with scales quite like this.

He held up the book. "Beautiful binding. Snake skin?"

Kabibble nodded. "From the Ghamkatchi Valley. The skins are wonderfully resilient, and the color stays vibrant for years."

Dover flipped through the book, which was ironically about snakes. There were no photographs, but the full color illustrations were amazingly lifelike. He paused to stare at one picture in particular. It was a snake, no doubt about that, but covered in fur instead of scales. He checked the title to see if it might be one of those *Ripley's Believe It Or Not* books. The gold foil stamp spelled out "Snakes of the Northern Territories." Interesting.

"Are you looking for something specific?" Kabibble asked, stretching over the counter to see Dover better, while keeping the rest of himself completely out of sight. "Or just browsing?"

Dover caught his bottom lip between his teeth, then said, "A little of both, I guess. Just killing time. You have anything about World War II?"

"You'll find the war books in the history section." Kabibble waved a hand at the last aisle. "Bottom shelf."

Dover stepped around the aisle's corner and leapt back when a round, furry object about the size of a saucer and just as flat scurried out from beneath a bookcase. It crossed Dover's path and slithered under one of two ragged armchairs set against a brick wall.

"What the hell was that?"

"What was what?" Kabibble peered where Dover pointed. "Was it round and flat with about a hundred legs, and did it hide under the chair?"

Dover nodded, breathing hard. It was the creepiest thing he'd ever seen. "It looked like a turtle with hair."

Kabibble grinned. "It's part turtle, part rat, and part centipede. I created him myself," he said proudly, then quickly added, "I should say 'it.' They're hermaphrodites."

Dover's eyes widened. "You're doing gene splicing experiments in a bookstore?"

"Of course not." Kabibble chuckled. "Simple alchemy is all. I call them skiddles 'cause of the way they move. They make great pets, and they eat all the silver fish and other nasty pests that could damage my inventory. They're shy creatures, but affectionate once they get to know you. Want me to call one out for you?" He stuck both little fingers in the corners of his mouth, preparing to whistle.

Dover shoved his hand out, palm forward. "No!"

"You sure? They'll crawl right onto your lap if you offer them a treat—"

Dover shook his head, feeling his gorge rise. "I'm sure they're very cuddly, but I think I'll pass."

Kabibble shrugged and went back to shuffling through the papers in front of him.

Giving the chair a wide berth, Dover checked the floor before continuing on.

He found very few books about war, and none of them had anything to do with World War II. In fact, he didn't recognize any of the wars spelled out in the titles, which were things like "The Battle of Harbvera's Twin Peaks" and "The War Between the Territories of Scavinos." The one called "Govotna's Fury: A Fight for Freedom" looked intriguing. He liked the title.

Again no photos, but lots of skillful drawings. This Govotna fellow wore peculiar armor that looked excessively heavy and allowed for an enormous hump on the man's back.

An advanced case of scoliosis, no doubt. Dover's cousin had it and needed surgery to prevent his acquiring a hump. Govotna must have waited too long.

"Find something?" Kabibble asked.

Dover stepped out from the aisle, hastening past the chair. "Yes, I think so," he said, brandishing Govotna's Fury for Kabibble to see.

The shopkeeper clapped his hands. "Excellent choice."

"How much?" Dover asked, sliding the wallet from his back pocket. "I have both Visa and MasterCard. Which do you prefer?"

Kabibble stared at him blankly.

"You do take credit cards, don't you? I rarely carry cash."

Looking sad, Kabibble shook his head. "I'm sorry, mister, uh..."

"Fisk," Dover said. "Handover Fisk, but everyone calls me Dover."

Kabibble looked pensive while saying, "Handover Fisk, Handover Fisk. Have you been in my shop before?"

Dover grinned. "I'd remember if so."

"How about your father? You named for him?"

"I share my dad's name, but he and my mom died twenty years ago, when I was six. I doubt you ever met him."

Kabibble sighed. "Ah, well. It'll come to me eventually. Now, about that Vizu and Mister Card—"

"Visa and MasterCard," Dover corrected. "They're credit cards. You mean you're not set up to accept credit cards? How do you stay in business?"

Kabibble spread his arms in a wide arc. "As you can see, I'm not packing them in. But I do okay."

"I don't have any cash on me."

"Have anything to trade?"

"Trade?" What an archaic method of exchange. It was obvious Kabibble wasn't from this country, though his English was flawless. Dover wondered how he ever managed to pay the shopping mall's exorbitant rent.

Kabibble reached over and tapped Dover's watch. "That should do just fine."

"You want my watch?" He began to peel the band from his wrist, thinking it was a good thing he'd left his Rolex at home. "Are you sure it's enough? This looks like an amazing book, a real work of art."

The old man cleared his throat and said, "You have a lot to learn about trading, Mr. Fisk. The object is to get the best deal, not necessarily the fairest one."

"Thanks for the advice," Dover said, then to himself, "I think."

"I'm having a sale on the thirteenth." Kabibble handed Dover a coupon. "Ten percent off everything in the store."

"But if your sales are made in trade—"

"You'll have to trust me."

"If you say so." Dover sidled to the door and grasped the handle.

"Tell all your friends about *Ish Kabibble's Books,*" the old man said. "Best books in the territories."

"I'll do that," Dover said. Territories? "I'll be back." He stepped outside and pulled the shop door closed, the bell issuing a muffled jingle behind him.

The alcove was dark, the jewelry store and baggage shop apparently having closed early. Odd for a weekend, Dover thought. But when he reached the mall's central thoroughfare, he discovered all the stores there were closed as well. He spun around, momentarily confused, and saw that the bookstore's lights were out and the display window seemed to fade as if clouded in mist. He rubbed his eyes, knowing he hadn't been in Kabibble's for more than an hour, but without his watch he wasn't completely certain. Nevertheless, there was no way the mall would close so early. He and Margie had yet to have dinner and see a movie; the last show was at eight o'clock. The mall always stayed open until nine. What the hell was going on?

A uniformed man turned the corner and headed in Dover's direction.

"Thank God," Dover said, rushing up to meet him.

"Stand back, sir," the security guard said, and washed his flashlight's beam over Dover from head to toe.

Dover flung a hand up to shield his eyes. "I didn't mean to stay inside the bookstore for so long."

"What bookstore?" the guard asked.

"The one back there." Dover gestured toward the alcove. "Next to the jewelry store. *Ish Kabibble's Books.*"

"There are no bookstores back there," the guard said, waving the flashlight where Dover had pointed. He steadied the beam. "See? It's a boarded up storefront. Nothing's been there since the hair salon that closed two years ago."

To Dover's amazement, the bookstore really was gone. Floor-to-ceiling sheets of plywood stood in its place, a FOR LEASE sign mounted on one of the boards. Dazed, Dover's knees felt as if they might melt. He staggered forward. "But I was just— I got this book—" He glanced at the book in his hands, relieved to see evidence that he hadn't lost his mind.

"Hold on there, buddy." The guard grabbed Dover's arm and led him to the bench that was no longer flanked by palm trees. They'd been replaced by pines covered with Christmas decorations.

"What the hell?" Dover murmured, his voice sounding thick inside his head.

"You're gonna be fine, sir," the guard told him. "Sit right here and put your head between your knees. Take some deep breaths and you'll feel lots better."

"You don't understand." Dover sat as instructed and heard ringing between his ears, a lot like the bookstore's bell above the door. "I was supposed to meet my wife for dinner and a movie. The mall shouldn't be closed yet. It hasn't even been an hour!"

The guard raised an eyebrow. "It's after three in the morning."

Dover gaped at him, too stunned to speak.

"What's your name, sir?"

"Fisk. Dover Fisk."

"Handover Fisk?"

Dover nodded.

The guard turned suddenly pale in the light of the Christmas Trees. "Holy shit."

"What's wrong?" Panic clutched Dover's heart. "Is it my wife? Has something happened to her?"

"Stay calm, Mr. Fisk." But the guard didn't sound too calm himself. His voice shook when he added, "Your wife is fine. But you..."

"I what?"

"You've been missing. When you didn't show up to meet your wife, she called mall security and we've kept an eye out for you ever since."

"How long ago was that?"

The guard swallowed. "You disappeared over a year ago."

* * *

Dover must have blacked out after hearing what the guard said. Either that, or the guard knocked him out. He vaguely remembered running back into the alcove where he'd first found *Ish Kabibble's Books*. He had banged his fists on the blank plywood walls where the store should have been. Dover now lay in a hospital bed and had no idea how he'd arrived there. He stared at his hands, which were bandaged, but they didn't hurt near as much as his head.

A man wearing a white coat entered the room and stopped by his bed. "I'm Dr. Anthony Dennis," the man said. "Are you feeling better, Mr. Fisk?"

Dover squinted up at him. "Not really. My head—"

"The security guard was over-zealous in apprehending you. He told me you'd gone completely berserk." Dr. Dennis tilted Dover's head forward and fingered the bandage in back. "Got quite an egg there. Swelling should go down in a day or two."

"Where's my wife? Where's Margie?"

The doctor patted his arm. "She's on her way. The ambulance arrived only a few hours ago. We couldn't call her until we confirmed who you were."

"What did she say?" Dover asked, feeling anxious. "Was she relieved to know I'm okay?"

The doctor patted his arm again. "I'll let her tell you. Rest until she gets here, all right?"

Dover's eyelids drooped, but he refused to give in to sleep. He had to tell Margie what had happened, where he'd been, all about Ish Kabibble and his skiddles, and the book bound in snake skin. He intended to show her the bookstore if only it hadn't disappeared minutes after he walked out. How did that happen? Dover flexed his fingers, feeling them throb within their bandages, testament to his futile attempt at trying to get through the plywood to reach the mysterious store that was no longer there.

He must have dozed off because it was his wife's voice that brought him back to consciousness. She was crying.

Poor Margie. She'd worried about him for over a year, not knowing if he were dead or alive. As far as she knew, he could have been mugged and left to die in the desert. Or maybe she thought he'd suffered from amnesia and only recently snapped out of it.

He reached for her hand. "Margie, I'm so sor—"

She yanked her hand away and slapped his face. "Bastard!"

Shocked, Dover said, "What? But I didn't—"

"How could you have left me like that?" She snatched a tissue from the box on the bedside table and dabbed her eyes. "I waited for you for hours. Mall security scoured every inch of every store looking for you, but you'd already run off to God knows where."

"Margie, that's not true. All I did was shop at a bookstore like you wanted me to."

"Liar!" She wiped her nose and made that infuriating pose of crossed arms pressed against her chest in defiance. "None of the clerks who worked at Borders that night ever saw you."

"That's because I didn't go there," Dover said, frustration making his voice squeak. "I went to an obscure book shop on the lower level—"

"Ish Kabibble's Books."

He brightened. "Yes!"

"No!" She lifted a phone book off the nightstand and dumped it on the bed. "I heard all about it from the security guard who found you, so I tried to look it up. It doesn't even exist!"

Dover chuckled. "Of course it exists, honey. I was there! The guy who runs it is so old fashioned he probably doesn't have a phone."

"I went back to the mall and looked for it myself," Margie said, her voice dripping with venom. "There is no Ish Kabibble, except for that old comedian's biography in Borders, and that guy's dead!"

Dover was furious with her lack of faith in him. He'd never lied to her and never would. "Say what you want, Margie, but Kabibble's store is real. I swear it on my life! I was in there for an entire year—" which seemed impossible, but must be true— "and that's the end of it!"

"I don't think so," she said with exaggerated sweetness. She pulled a manila envelope from her bag and threw it at him. "This is."

"What's that?"

"Divorce papers." Her arms recrossed and she leveled him with a chilly glare.

"Margie, sweetheart. Please don't do this to us."

She screeched a laugh. "Why not? *You* had no problem walking out on me, leaving me with unpaid bills and a mortgage out the wazoo! I had to file bankruptcy, then get a job—me, a job!—just to keep the house. I searched everywhere for you, Dover, and so did the FBI. Only recently were you declared dead so that I could cash in your life insurance policy and get on with *my* life, but now you suddenly show up—" She exploded in a renewed torrent of tears.

So that's why Margie was so upset. It wasn't because she felt betrayed by Dover, or because she'd been out of her mind with worry. Nothing so innocent. She was upset because he'd spoiled her plan for a $250,000 payoff. She didn't give a damn about him.

"Jerk!" Margie snatched up the divorce papers and smacked his leg with them. "I'm taking you for all I can get!" She spun around and sashayed out the door, wiggling her bouncy little bottom behind her.

Once she was out of his room, Dover climbed from the bed and held onto the bedside table. Still dizzy from his bump on the noggin, he used the wheeled table for balance while making his way to the window.

Looking down on the line of parked cars along the street, he watched Margie leap into the arms of a man he didn't recognize. This came as no big surprise after what she'd just told him. And Dover's heart didn't ache near as much as it should have, which said a lot about their marriage.

"Bitch," he murmured, still watching the couple in their lovers' clinch before they indulged in a languorous kiss. He shut his eyes, unable to watch anymore.

Dr. Dennis came in and asked, "So how did it go?"

Dover held up the divorce papers.

The doctor grimaced. "I was afraid of that. She sounded pretty angry on the phone." He cleared his throat. "Now we need to concentrate on getting you well enough to return to society."

Confused, Dover said, "Excuse me?"

"Please understand, Mr. Fisk, that I don't want to keep you here, but under the circumstances—"

"What circumstances?"

"No one's seen or heard from you in over a year. You may have blocked out all memory of that time, suffered amnesia caused by either trauma or a blow to the head. You'll need neurological tests followed by psychotherapy."

Dover sat on the bed and stared solemnly at the doctor. "You don't believe me either."

Dr. Dennis narrowed his eyes while studying him, as if considering the possibility he could be telling the truth. "You and I will talk, Mr. Fisk." He winked at Dover and headed for the door, but before leaving he added, "We'll get to the bottom of this."

Dover felt on the verge of tears. How could something like this happen to him? He'd led a decent, ordinary life up to this point. Had a good job with a prosperous accounting firm, lived in a nice home in the suburbs, was married to a beautiful woman who loved him, or so he had thought. And just because of some arcane little bookstore no one ever heard of that was run by an eccentric old man who bred creatures called skiddles—

"The book," he said, glancing around the room. "Where's the book?" He slid off the bed and opened the nightstand drawer to search for his copy of *Govotna's Fury: A Fight For Freedom*. But the drawers were empty. He went to the closet beside the bathroom and flung open the door. His clothes were folded neatly on the top shelf, the exact same clothing he'd worn on that fateful night at the mall over a year ago. That alone must prove he was telling the truth. He lifted the flannel shirt and khaki trousers from the shelf, finding the book underneath.

"So I'm not crazy," he whispered to himself, because he'd begun to have doubts. After all, there was no logical explanation for an hour's worth of book browsing somehow expanding into more than a year. Preposterous. But undeniably true.

He hugged *Govotna's Fury* to his chest, then laid it gently on the bed. There was no other book like it in the world. He realized that now, and he also realized Kabibble was just as unique.

Dover yanked his pants on. He fished through the pockets until he found Kabibble's coupon announcing the store's sale on the thirteenth. *The thirteenth of what?*

He heard footsteps in the hall, so he jumped into bed, ignoring the hammers of pain inside his skull. He shoved his shirt and the book beneath the covers, making sure his clothed legs were hidden as well.

A female nurse wearing a patronizing smile entered the room. "How are you this afternoon, Mr. Fisk?"

"Great. Terrific." He sounded jumpy, but he couldn't help it.

The woman scowled. "A bit agitated, are we? A nice sedative will fix you right up." She handed him a paper cup that held two little blue pills.

Dover pretended to swallow the pills, but shoved them between his gum and cheek instead.

Measuring his words so they wouldn't come out too fast, he asked, "What's today's date?"

The woman's smile broadened. "Less than two weeks until Christmas. Hopefully, you'll be home by then."

"The date?" he pressed.

"December thirteenth."

Gratified by her answer, Dover smiled back. "Thank you." Those two words—*December thirteenth*—were like a subliminal trigger. Kabibble's sale was today. In his mind's eye, Dover saw Kabibble's gray eyes sparkle with what might be a summons, and he knew he had to get back to the store. Maybe the old man could reverse time, give him his old life back, and Margie... Well, knowing what he knew now about Margie, that part of his life would have to change.

* * *

Between bus rides and walking, it took Dover almost two hours to reach the shopping mall. His panic level remained high even though he had successfully escaped from the hospital by sneaking down the back stairs. Now inside the mall, he walked casually through the lane of brightly lit stores, *Govotna's Fury* pressed close to his body to conceal his heaving chest.

He tried to breath calmly, telling himself everything would be fine once he reached Kabibble's store. When he passed the arcade, he quickened his pace. The same base-pounding music boomed through the doors as it had last night. No, he corrected himself. Last *year*. When he smelled the popcorn, his heart began to race. He was almost there. He saw the bluish glow emanating from the jewelry store's display window, and just as he reached the corner before the alcove...

"Mr. Fisk?" came a voice from behind him. "Please stop right there, Mr. Fisk. I want to help you."

Dover glanced over his shoulder and saw the same guard who had accosted him the night before. He reflexively touched the bandage on the back of his head.

"Real sorry about that, sir," the guard said, walking slowly toward him. "You were acting crazy the way you kept banging on that wall and yelling 'Ish Kabibble, let me in!' over and over. I was afraid you'd hurt yourself."

Dover lunged around the corner and ran.

He heard footsteps gaining quickly behind him, but that didn't matter because right in front of him was *Ish Kabibble's Books*. Tears of relief sprang to his eyes as the shop door loomed a hundred yards ahead, the OPEN sign like a gift from God. He thought the guard would stop chasing him once he saw the store, but the rapid patter of footfalls only grew louder.

Dover expected to feel the guard's large, rough hands on his neck at any second. His heart beat so hard and fast he felt sure it would explode, and he gasped air into lungs that burned like fire. His hand only inches from the door knob, he felt certain the guard's breath had just brushed his right ear. Then the door suddenly swung inward. Dover fell through it, landing in a sprawled heap on the floor.

"I knew you'd come back," Ish Kabibble said, slamming the door in the guard's startled face. But there was no calamitous thud of the guard's body against the door, nor a rattle of the display window on impact. Only the jingle of the tiny silver bell that announced a customer had just dropped in.

Dover held onto his chest, panting so hard his eyes bulged with each breath. He remained on the floor, staring in shock at Kabibble, who stood on two bestial legs covered with fur. What new horror was this? The old man's black hooves clacked across the tiles as he returned to the sales counter, his ringed, cat-like tail wagging behind him.

Dover fought for each breath, his throat on the verge of collapsing. "What— What—?"

"Dear boy, please settle down," Kabibble said. He handed him a cup. "Drink this."

Dover grabbed it and gulped the liquid down. Water. Cool, sweet water.

Kabibble splayed his hands by his sides and peered down at himself. "Not something you see every day, eh?"

All Dover could do was stare.

"Sorry about the shock, however I had no choice but to let you see all of me this time." He tossed a quick look at the door.

Dover guzzled the rest of the water, his breathing finally starting to slow. "What about—?"

"Your friend out there?" Kabibble chuckled, which made his tail bounce. "The store disappeared from view the second I shut the door."

"But did he see it?"

"He saw it, all right. I'm not sure how much he'll remember once he regains consciousness, though." Kabibble tilted his head at the door and grinned. "He ran quite a header into that plywood."

Now that Dover's composure had returned, recent events made an odd sort of sense. It was clear that Kabibble had known all along what would happen to him. He'd known nobody would believe there had ever been a store called *Ish Kabibble's Books*. He'd known Dover would come back, *have* to come back, just to prove his own sanity. And he'd known the guard, or some other authority figure, would try to stop him.

The heat of anger made Dover's ears burn. He clambered to his knees. "You son-of-a-bitch."

Kabibble backed toward his counter. "Now, sonny, hold on. I know you're upset and I understand. I have some things I need to tell you."

Dover was on his feet now and hadn't heard a word Kabibble had said. His life was totally ruined, all because of this ancient freak and his bizarre bookstore.

"Mr. Fisk," Kabibble said. "Dover. Stop and listen to me."

Dover grabbed the lapels of Kabibble's checkered sports jacket. The two were at eye level with each other, and for the moment Dover forgot about the hoofed feet he stood toe-to-toe with. In fact, he drew Kabibble so close their noses almost touched and he felt the strange man's loops of earrings brush across his knuckles.

Through teeth gritted shut, Dover said, "You destroyed my life."

In an icy tone Dover had never heard uttered from a human mouth, Kabibble said, "You didn't have much of one to destroy."

Dover was about to respond when he noticed Kabibble's eyes flash. There was fury in that flash, and also wisdom, courage, honor. Dover let him go.

"Now will you listen to reason?" Kabibble straightened his jacket and shot his cuffs. Shoulders pulled back, he returned to his sales counter, his bobbing tail in contrast to his dignity.

Dover shut his eyes and heaved a sigh so deep it practically lifted him on his toes. "I'm sorry, Kabibble. That was completely out of character for me."

"I doubt you have any idea what your character is."

The statement surprised Dover and he laughed. "You talk as if you know me."

"In a way, I do know you," Kabibble said. "Remind me again when you last saw your father."

Dover frowned at the sudden change of subject. "When I was six. Like I told you before, that's when he and my mother died. It was a train accident in the tube between London and Liverpool."

Kabibble shook his head, his expression dubious. "Tragic. Were their bodies ever found?"

"No." Still frowning, Dover said, "I don't know what any of this has to do with—"

"Humor me." Kabibble laced his fingers together and rested his chin on the knuckly pillow. "Where were they going when the accident happened?"

"Shopping." Dover grew impatient. "After they were killed, I was sent to live with my aunt and uncle here in the states. End of story."

"It would seem so, wouldn't it?" Kabibble gave Dover an appraising look. "I should have recognized you right off when you came in the first time. My shop only appears for those with an adventurous heart—"

Dover barked a laugh. "Me, adventurous? You've got to be kidding."

"Don't interrupt," Kabibble snapped. "It's rude. Where was I? Oh, yes. Well, that's your father, an adventurous heart. When he and your mother stepped into my shop twenty years ago, they had no idea what wondrous experiences awaited them, but it came with a price. They had to make a choice."

Dover grabbed one of the bookshelves to steady himself. "My parents are alive?"

"Oh, yes," Kabibble said. "Very much so. Once I made the connection with your name, I spoke to your father last night and told him I'd met you. He's eager to see you again."

"Hold it." Dover felt suddenly dizzy. He wanted to believe the old man, but what Kabibble just said was impossible. Then again, the realm of possibility apparently had no boundaries. "Why didn't my parents take me with them twenty years ago?"

"Ah, now that's a sticky point. A price paid for the choice made." Kabibble scratched his chin, appearing deep in thought. "You see, boy, when your parents were offered a chance to cross the territory gateway between dimensions, time in your part of the world had spun ahead five years. You were already comfortably ensconced in your new life in America. So it was either unveil the fable of your parents' presumed deaths and thrust you into a life-altering media frenzy, or leave well enough alone."

Dover understood. "You're saying time runs totally different in our two worlds?"

Kabibble nodded.

"And that's why over a year passed out there while I spent less than an hour here in your store."

Again Kabibble nodded.

"So that means if I walked out right now, it wouldn't be today anymore."

Kabibble checked a pocket watch that hung from a chain attached to his lapel. "In this time zone—there are hundreds, you know—close to a year has already passed. Which isn't so bad. You can leave now if you like. Assume a new identity, get another job with another accounting firm, be married again, live in a comfortable home in the suburbs." Kabibble rolled his eyes. "Exactly like what you had before."

Dover's old life didn't sound so appealing anymore. It sounded, well, boring. He glanced around the shop, at the books lined up on the shelves, their fascinating contents a bare glimpse into an exotic world that could be his to explore. To explore with his father.

"I'm staying," Dover announced.

"Excellent decision! Your father will be pleased."

"Where, exactly, is my father?"

"Not in here, I can assure you," Kabibble said. "He and your mother move around a lot. You might call them nomads."

"Then how will I find them?"

"Not to worry, my boy. There are ways."

Kabibble laid a parental hand on Dover's shoulder and led him to the back of the shop. He whistled and the sound of thousands of tiny feet scampered across the floor toward them.

"Did I ever tell you what great travel companions my skiddles are? No? Well, they're very quick and quite strong for their size. I have this wonderful chariot that I hitch them to, and they run like the wind. Cost? What do you have to trade, my boy? The book you bought from me last night? That will serve as a down payment, but once you reach your father, I'll expect something more. Perhaps one of the delicious kapootny pies your mother is so skilled at baking..."

The End

About the Author:

Karen Duvall challenges the ethics of human cryonics in her supernatural thriller, Project Resurrection, which is currently under consideration with a Hollywood production company for a made-for-TV movie. A winner of two regional writing awards, Karen writes stories that blur the boundaries of reality and challenge the imagination. Karen lives in Evergreen, Colorado with her husband and teenage daughter, and is currently working on a paranormal mystery series set on the Big Island of Hawaii.

karenduvall@echelonpress.com
http://www.karenduvall.com

Book Work

Lazette Gifford

Book Work

A whisper of sound, leather brushing against wood, drew my attention to see the little book once again trying to work it's way out from underneath the five heavier tomes I had piled atop it.

"Oh no you don't!" I made a very unladylike leap from my chair, and grabbed the cover before it got away. The book fluttered wildly before realizing it could lose a page or two, and then settled reluctantly in my hand. I didn't want to know what mischief it had planned this time!

Although I had been pleased to find the small book back in a dusty corner of the library, I now wondered if the few pages of enigmatic notes on the Battle of Frog Pond were worth the trouble the book created. The notes covered hardly a handful of pages, after all, while the rest were filled with wizardly scribbling. I wasn't interested in the magic sections. I wanted to be a historian, not a witch, much to the chagrin of my parents.

However, that didn't mean I couldn't appreciate a good spell. The Frogs-to-Princes enchantment that ended the Battle of Frog Pond had been masterly. Unfortunately, like most truly spectacular spells, it had created a serious problem all it's own. In this case the difficulty started with one hundred identical young men, all of whom thought they were the heir to the throne. If it hadn't been that they occasionally croaked—the sound, that is—it would have been impossible to tell any of them were imposters. And people did still wonder what happened to the real prince...and the wizard who had messed with the lives of some now rather unhappy frogs. I had heard from my mother—a healing witch who occasionally worked in the palace—that once a frog prince became convinced he wasn't the real thing, the spell broke and he happily hopped away out to the nearest cache of water. That, unfortunately, often turned out to be the fountain in the courtyard, and ambassadors were starting to complain about the noise at night.

The more I delved into the research on the now five-year-long animal wars, the more I became convinced that all our trouble with the other creatures had started with that spell. It was no wonder the mage had disappeared.

Some people didn't take the war very seriously in the first two years, although after Snail Siege only fools weren't careful of where they stepped.

I intended to write a history of those years—a readable history, as opposed to Agalitine's plodding opus that might, if produced in enough numbers, make better bricks than books. I'd been working on it for months already. I wanted the book done by the anniversary of the Battle of Bat Cave, so I could present it to the King and whatever Prince heir had taken over at that point. It would be my big moment, and I hadn't time to waste.

But the little book kept drawing my attention by flapping covers, or throwing itself over the top of whatever I tried to read. I petted it now and then, telling the poor little thing what a fine binding and excellent paper it had. However, the one time I had become so engrossed in my work that it got away, it knocked over a nearby display of weasel art. I very nearly got kicked out of the library for that one. After all, you don't want to piss off the weasels.

The book and I were obviously going to have to come to an understanding. "Tell me what you want," I said, letting the pages ruffled under my hands. I almost felt sorry for the little thing. After all, it had no name, no author-parent, and a lot of energy for something barely larger than my hand.

I began to flip through the pages again, ignoring all the wizardly things that took up most of the first half. I hadn't noticed the words scrawled in on the edges here and there, but they didn't interest me.

The pages ruffled, and dropped open to a page of spells. I turned past it. It turned back. I tried again, but obviously the book wanted me to see something here.

I scanned the spells, but they looked pretty pedestrian. Then I saw, cramped down in the lower corner by the binding, something written in very small letters. Intrigued, I pulled the book up close to my nose.

"Is this it?" I said. The page did stay still this time.

> *"I wish that my own true love*
> *Would come to me on the wings of a dove*
> *Flying through the boundless sky*
> *And calling to me with a sweet dove cry."*

I grimaced. Poetry had never been my favorite genre, and this one sounded a bit sophomoric, at best. I shook my head and put the book down on the table... And that was when I realized that what I read wasn't a poem. I had just read a spell. Aloud.

"Shi-coo!"

The world changed that quickly. I had been a young woman intent on my studies in one moment, the next I found myself flapping up to the highest shelf in a flutter of bird-like panic.

I was a dove. Oh damn, oh damn.

"Coo-ah, coo, coo, coo."

Probably just as well that I couldn't speak. I had learned some very bad words from my older brothers. The damned book had remained on the table, and I swept down with the intention of pecking holes in every word. It panicked before I got close enough, and leapt under the table.

I started to head for the librarian, but stopped myself out of sheer embarrassment. They let me have full run of the library because I supposedly knew better than to read a spell and get transformed. Besides, I knew the librarian could do nothing for me. I'd have to go to someone with real magical powers and show them what had happened. I hoped it wasn't one of those spells that could only be undone by the person who made it.

I would need the spell to get help, so I dropped to the floor and darted under the table, grabbing the cover with my talons. The thing felt heavier than I expected, but I managed to reach the top of the bookcase and look for an inconspicuous way out of the building.

There—up through the grate by the window where a spell kept things from coming in. However, those types of enchantments were directional, and had no trouble getting out, though it was a tight fit.

I sailed up into the sky. When my companion protested, I landed in a tree and pecked the cover several times until it settled down. We were finally coming to an understanding.

The world looked very odd from up here, and my sight focused on different things. That cherry way up in the boughs looked delicious, so I had a bit of a snack before we moved on.

I started to fly toward home, but I suddenly felt as though I moved through treacle. I barely reached the next tree, exhausted and panting. I found myself pounding the book against a limb out of pure frustration, but stopped before I did it any real harm.

And I felt—like I had flown in the wrong direction. So I turned and flew back to the first tree. Odd how much easier that proved to be. Invigorating, in fact. I swept past the tree and turned toward the city—and hit treacle again. Back to the tree and another direction—no go. But if I flew on in the same direction I had been, it filled my entire (albeit small) body with an exhilaration I had never known before. Even the book felt light in my hands—ah, claws.

I headed toward the sea...

I don't know if doves usually fly for great distances, but I made it all the way across the Artan Strait and on to the Parish Isles. I had hoped whatever drew me would be at North Isle, or the nice sea resort on Fallintinicis. But no, of course not. Instead we went to Bleak Island, and the prison.

This didn't really surprise me, given the way things had gone so far. I tried to fly past, but there was no use. I circled around, following the easy path until I landed at the high window of a small, dark cell.

"Coo?"

The book tried desperately to get away. I pounded it against the bar, but that seemed to have awakened something inside. The book and I both went still at a growl of sound and movement, a shadow in shadows. The thing looked small and hairy, and came toward the window with an inhuman gait—

No. It came at the window with a bad limp, and it—he— looked as though he hadn't seen a razor or a bath in quite a while. Nor much other care, either, from what I could tell. And this, I realized with a soft coo, had to be the person who created the spell.

"What have we here?" he said, a soft whisper of words in

the dark. Pretty voice, interesting accent. Not a local, then. "Lovely bird. Don't worry, I won't hurt you. Nice to see anything visit, though I fear I haven't any crumbs to share."

Well, you know, how could I be angry with someone half starved who wished he had crumbs to give me?

"Coo," I said. Damn.

"How is the day out there? I can't reach the bars, I fear. They won't let me see the sky any more."

Damn, damn, damn! "Coo!"

I began working my way through those bars, pulling the book in with me. He sure better have an antidote for the spell, or we were going to have a long dove-to-human discussion about what he'd done. And he would understand me, even if I had to peck the words out on his arm.

"You don't want to come in here," he said, and sounded a little worried. Given the situation in the world these days, it was always wise to be wary of an animal acting oddly.

However, I made it through with only the loss of a few feathers and swept down at him. He dropped to the floor and cowered into the corner. I threw the damn book at him. I was tempted to drop something else on him as well, but refrained.

"Ow!" he yelped. And then his breath caught in a sound of surprise. "Oh!"

I settled onto the cold, stone floor before him as he picked up the book. He looked like someone who had just been reunited with a long lost child. He held the book to his chest and bowed his head, and I waited with more patience than I thought I would have had at this point.

"I don't understand," he finally said. Cultured voice, I realized, and that meant he was probably a political prisoner. I wondered what he'd done, and what trouble I had walked—ah, flew—into. "Why would a bird bring me my book? How could you know?"

"Coo, coo, coo!"

"I wish I could understand you, my friend. I owe you a debt of gratitude. This is the first hope I've had of escape in many years."

Years? He wasn't that old. "Coo?"

He began just fluttering through the pages. I wanted to go and yank the book out of his hand and show him the proper page, but he looked like someone who had just had redemption handed to him on a golden platter. I found it inexplicably pleasing to see him reading through pages, stopping now and then to nod, and a moment or two to wipe tears from his eyes.

So I settled down on a bit of old straw by the door. The door, I noted, had not been opened in a long time. I could see a small hole through which someone pushed food, and I did find a crumb there after all. There was a privy of sorts in the far corner, but it was little more than a hole in the floor. It did not look like a very good place to have lived for years.

The sun began to drift down, and reddish light illuminated the cell. My nameless companions—man and book—moved with the light, trying to capture as much of the day as they could while he read. I just sighed and waited.

And then, in the last of the sunlight—

"Oh. Oh dear. The dove spell."

That picked up my attention right away. I flapped my wings and scooted, more than flew, closer to him. He had the page open, though I could barely see the words in the falling light. I reached over and pecked at it in anger.

"Yes, I see. Oh dear. We do have a problem."

I pecked his hand. He yelped and pulled back, looking startled. I felt badly for a moment, but panic had gotten the better of me. He wasn't making any sort of sounds like he could get me out of this damn dove body. I started to flap my wings as well, and my coos got a bit louder and more caw-like.

"Calm, calm!" he said. "We have a problem, but it's something I can fix! I could change you back with a kiss. Sorry it's so melodramatic, but I was a silly child when I wrote that. Teenage angst and all of that sort of thing."

I looked up into his face. He had very pretty green eyes beneath a fall of dirty brown hair. "Coo?"

"Oh, I don't mind kissing you," he said. His hand brushed over my head, and by the Gods, my heart pounded at that soft touch. "But then what would you do?"

"Coo!" I looked around the cell. He was right. Damn, damn, damn!

"I can see only one way out of this, my friend. I'm sorry you got dragged into my mess, but now we'll have to work together if either of us hopes to get free. I'm going to study my book tomorrow. I remember a spell or two in here that I think I can use to get us out of here. I may need you to bring me a few supplies, though. I promise I will do my best to make certain you are set to right as soon as I can. And I do apologize."

"Coo," I sighed. I could see no choice, really.

The sunlight had nearly gone, but he slid with it still, holding the book in his hands. When the last of the light faded, he leaned against the wall with the book in his hands and pressed it to his chest. Hope.

I did wish I knew why he was in prison. I hated the thought that I might help free someone who shouldn't be let lose among the people. I mean a wizard of power—and this young? I didn't sleep well that night. I didn't sleep much at all, in fact.

* * *

At dawn I pushed my way back out of the bars and went

looking for a little food. Bleak Island is well named, by the way. It's a pile of rock, with smaller rocks and pinnacles all around it, making it hard for anyone to get to the shore except at the tiny port. Seagulls screamed through the skies and eyed me as an intruder, but left me alone. I did finally locate a garden that must have belonged to the warden. There I ate a couple lovely berries, and tried to pull a tomato free to take back to my new friend. When the door to the building opened, I dropped down into the bush, quivering, but silent.

"Yeah, old Turnstone says he felt some surge of magic last night. I thought at worst it was another ant invasion, but he says this was human made. We need to get the old guy replaced, Warden. He couldn't track it. I've taken the liberty of calling Bullock in from Fallintinicis. He'll be here tomorrow."

"Very good."

I looked out from among the leaves and saw two men. One wore a dark gray uniform that made him a prison guard. The other, in a blue tunic and trousers, had the coldest, meanest eyes I had ever seen. He had to be the warden.

"If there is magic involved, we know who is behind it, don't we?" the man said.

"Yes sir. Pretty obvious that it has to be Andoni since we don't have any other wizard prisoners, and except for old Turnstone, no one else on the island knows magic at all. I don't know how he could have managed, though."

"Neither do I, but a wizard of his ability is always dangerous. I wish the general would give us leave to kill him and be done with it, but he thinks there might be counter spells set that would trigger at his death. Still, we can take precautions short of that. Be certain that he is in no condition for magic today, will you?"

"Yes sir."

The guard left. I sat in the bush, wishing the warden away so that I could fly out. I had to warn Andoni!

But I couldn't escape without drawing attention, and a dove here... no, that would be too obvious. The warden worked in his garden for quite some time, whistling tunelessly as he pulled weeds and trimmed herbs, unconcerned with what his guard did. I wanted to go and peck his eyes out! But I stayed very still, sliding back into the shadows only when he came closer.

He finally left, but by then I feared going back to the cell for fear of what I might find there. I slipped out of the tomato bush and forced myself to fly back, staying in the shadows, and afraid of this Turnstone, wherever he might be.

I found the book cowering on the window ledge, just outside the bars. The poor thing looked terrified, but that ended one of my fears. The guard hadn't found the book, and we still had hope. I patted it with a wing, peered inside to make sure the guard had gone, and then pushed it back through.

Andoni lay quite still in a corner by the door. I suppressed a startled coo and flapped down to him, and the book came with me. I nudged Andoni's hand, and he made a sound, as though swallowing off the show of pain. But he lifted his head. I could see blood on his lips, but he still smiled.

"There you are. I feared you would come back too soon. Don't fret. I'll be fine. This isn't the first time."

Moving proved difficult for him, and I feared broken ribs, though they were likely only bruised. His hands looked worse though. I hoped they weren't broken.

"They know there is magic on the island. Not surprising since even something as small as the two of you are beacons in a place with no magic at all. We don't have time to be subtle, Dove. Sorry—that's what I'll have to call you for now."

I bobbed my head several times. Fine. I didn't care. I just wanted to get him out of here... so that I could be saved from the spell, of course.

He could hardly even lift the book, but a moment of worry passed when I realized the pages turned for him, and he looked quite intent on the work. So I sat in a corner and waited. Soon he began sending me out for supplies. Most I found locally: twigs, rocks, and sand that I gathered in a piece of cloth torn from his ragged tunic. However, I had to go all the way to Fallintinicis for the gold thread. Apparently being sent by the person who cast the spell eased the treacle feeling to the air, but it still took me all the rest of the morning to reach the island. Then I spent several more hours fluttering around the tailor's street, trying to find a long piece of gold thread that a dove might easily grab. I caused a bit of a stir when I did, but determination got me away again.

I was so tired that I rested part way back on the main arm of a sailing ship heading in the right direction. It felt wonderful to give my wings a rest, and I think I would have napped right then, if a man hadn't come racing up to the deck, yelling to someone behind him.

"No, there is something magical here! I can feel it. I thought the warden and Turnstone were crazy, but I think—"

I had swept straight up into the sky before I heard any more. The ship couldn't be more than three hours from docking. We didn't have much time.

Andoni was asleep when I arrived. I knew he needed the rest, but I flew over and dropped the thread beside the other items, and then gently pushed at his hand. He moaned and I regretted it, but he came awake.

"Ah. Back." I thought he looked a little uncertain this time, as though he had forgotten what he was doing. The book sat in his lap. I leapt up on his leg and nudged it. He looked down and nodded. "Yes, I know. We need to work."

I flapped my wings. And then I flapped them frantically.

"Quickly? Is there trouble coming?"

I nodded, bobbing my head several times.

"Ah. Well, I guess it won't do to rest for awhile then," he said. He sounded very tired, and when he moved, it was like someone very old. Or very hurt. "I'm going to make a gate—"

"Coo!"

"Yes, I know. I hardly have the energy to sustain something that powerful. We'll only get one chance."

I fluttered around, worried and wishing I could say so. *A gate!* That took powerful, dangerous magic. I thought he had just planned to blow the door open or something—but now I realized how useless that would be. Where would he go from there? He couldn't fight his way out, and even if he kissed me, I wasn't trained in weapons, even providing I could find one.

So I settled down by the door, watching silently while he laid out all the supplies. His hands shook with the effort, and my heart pounded so hard that I could barely stay still. Even the book trembled, but kept its page and moved now and then at Andoni's direction. After awhile his slow movements and whispered words lulled me into sleep.

* * *

I awoke with a hand clamped around my body, and my head pressed into some cloth. I started to fight, panicked that we had been found.

"Calm," Andoni whispered. "I'm almost done with the base for the gate, but I can hear someone coming. Be calm and quiet, Dove."

I obeyed. I could hear the sound of voices outside the door. Had the wizard from the ship arrived? I didn't know how long I had slept, but it must have been quite some time since I could see that Andoni had built a complex set of runes on the floor, overlapping and circled by the golden thread. I thought it glowed with power even now.

"I have a chant, Dove, that I must do and cannot be stopped, or else all is lost." He looked frantically toward the door. "I won't make it. There's no time. Go. Fly. I'll try to break the spell. I think I can do that even if—all else is lost."

He had started to say even if he died. No.

I pulled away from him, and perched on the ledge above the door.

"You can't help."

"Coo ah, coo, coo, coo!"

He started to argue, but the book banged him in the leg. He looked down at the runes and then gave a little shrug. "I've nothing to lose. But you, Dove—"

"Coo!"

"Yes. No time."

He started chanting. The language of magic is lovely and melodious, and reminded me of home. They would be worried by now—but soon we would be in my parent's house. I would take Andoni to my mother. She would help heal him.

As he spoke, one rune after another began to glow.

"Yes! There's an increase in magic! Get this open!"

I heard someone lifting a bar from the far side of the door. The bird part of me wanted to fling myself across the room and out the window, but I didn't do more than move from foot-to-foot, and wait.

"Careful, Warden," someone said. "Magic that strong— no telling what he has waiting for us!"

Good. Let them worry. Let them take their time. Another rune glowed, and the next. Only two remained, and I knew enough about magic to see that he only needed a moment longer, and the gate would be created.

The door opened an inch, another. A sword tip appeared.

I screamed and threw myself out the door at the men. I hoped it didn't upset Andoni's magic, but I suspected someone as good as him would need far more than a noise to upset him.

I flew straight into the face of the first man, and he screamed as well. I clawed him, and swooped up before the Warden could grab me. Then I dived at them again, driving both back from the door by the sheer insanity of my attack, one dove against two full-grown men.

But it worked. I heard the gate opening in the cell. There is nothing in the world that sounds quite like it: a hum that could be a choir of gods, singing to the world.

"Dove!" Andoni yelled. "Come on!"

I swept around and headed back to the door, folding my wings and gliding through—but not fast enough. Someone grabbed my tail feathers and I screamed in pain and fear—

Andoni stood at the edge of a gate that glowed like a thousand candles. He was pale white and swaying with weakness, but he still reached, and would not go without me.

And I couldn't get free of the guard who had clamped a hand around my body, and reached to snap my neck.

"No!" Andoni yelled. He stepped away from the gate, ready to help me.

Book leapt out of Andoni's hands and hit the guard fully in the face. The man didn't just let go of me: he threw me across the room. I saw Andoni reaching for me, but he tripped and fell through the portal.

He and the portal disappeared in the next heartbeat.

Well, that was a fine mess. I had no idea where he'd gone. All I knew was that the guard had begun beating the book against the wall, and it flapped feebly, the binding bent and tearing. I screeched and attacked again. He dropped the book and I grabbed it in mid air. Neat trick that. I could get used to being a dove, I suppose.

I headed for the window and got us through before they could catch us. I flew straight out into the sea. I put miles and miles between us and that horrible place, hoping the wizard could not track magic that far.

We finally found a haven of rocky outcroppings in the midst of the ocean. The gulls watched us suspiciously, and I don't know if they realized I was—or had been—a human. Book and I curled up on the lee side of a rock and slept for the night.

* * *

The next day the rocks sat enshrouded in a fog. I woke up and shook the water from my feathers, watching with distaste as the gulls feasted on some nasty smelling fish. I feared there wasn't a nut or berry anywhere for miles. I was quite hungry, too.

Book fluttered a bit beneath me, trying to shake water off as well, poor thing. I wiped it with a wing, and it snuggled in closer. The gulls seemed a little more curious now, and I really didn't want to sit around waiting for them to decide they didn't like me. Besides, I noticed a school of angry looking tuna making their way toward the rocks, and I suspected there was going to be quite a row before too long.

I picked up the book and lifted into the sky, wondering which way I should go. The fog made me fear that heading the wrong way would put us too far out at sea to find any safety.

I fluttered around in a circle...

Treacle, treacle, free sailing.

I gave a cry of delight. I knew now I would find Andoni

again, no matter how far he'd gone.

* * *

We reached the mainland just before dark. I wanted to see Andoni yet tonight, if he wasn't too far. I realized that my parents would be frantic by now, and that I would have to confess my stupidity to them after all. It wasn't a pleasant thought, but maybe I'd grown up a little in the last few days. I knew, after seeing Andoni in that cell, that there was far worse that could happen to a person than a little embarrassment.

I only hoped that Andoni hadn't been in that prison for a very good reason. That still played at the back of my mind, worrying me as I flew on. I went over the library, past the street where I lived, and on—

Castle?

Yes, castle. I had started past, but the pull drew me back down into the courtyard, where some pigeon guards took offense at my appearance. Up book and I went again, with the birds yelling complaint.

I found a balcony with doors open into a large room, filled with fine furniture. The first person I saw was my mother, mixing something by a table. I nearly squeaked with joy. Someone else sat by the bed, and yet another rested within it, braced by pillows and covered in blankets. They did not hear me come sweeping in.

"Father had General Telski arrested already. And he's sent a troop ship off to Bleak. You're safe now."

"If they killed her— Gods, Farlis, how could I have gone off and left them!"

"You had no choice. And you're lucky you're alive to tell me about it."

Two things registered almost at once. One was that Farlis was the long lost *real* Prince Heir—easy to tell because he didn't croak at all when he talked. He didn't seem to be very lost to me, sitting here in his own castle. And the one in the

120

bed was Andoni.

"Coo ah!"

He sat straight up. I dropped the book into his lap, and settled on the bed beside him.

"Praise the Gods! It's Dove!"

"I rather figured it must be," Farlis said. My mother came over looking a little curious, and then amused. I would have blushed, but was saved that by being a dove.

Adoni looked better with his hair washed and brushed out, his face shaved, although there were bruises and cuts everywhere, and his hand shook as he patted Book with the fondness some people shower on their cats. And then he reached out a bandaged hand to me, and I carefully climbed up on it.

"Dove, I never would have gotten out of there without you. 'Thank you' seems insufficient."

I seriously considering pecking his nose when he pulled me close and kissed me.

Well, that proved interesting. I went from dove to human again, and not quite small enough to hold on his hand. Instead, I had a very lovely human male underneath me—and my mother watching. We both looked quite surprised, staring into each other's eyes.

"Well," Prince Farlis said.

"Your Highness!" I scrambled off the bed. Still clothed, I was glad to see. It could have been worse.

"You know who I am?" he said, and looked troubled.

"This, Prince Farlis, is my missing daughter," my mother said. She came and embraced me. "I could sense you with magic, and knew you were safe enough—but I had no idea what had happened. From all I've heard, you did very well, child."

"I did something stupid," I said. Better to confess now and get it over with. "I read something from an obviously magical book without even considering it."

"Well, you wouldn't be the first one," she said, with a glint in her eyes that made me want to ask what silliness she had done in her youth. But she turned back to Andoni and gently pushed him against the pillows again. "You can stop worrying. Lefreeanna will be quite easy to find. We live at the foot of Foxglove Road."

"Lefreeanna?" Andoni said, looking at me.

"You can call me Dove," I said, and sat in a chair on the other side of the bed. I felt exhausted. "May I ask what's going on? Why are you here? "

Andoni smiled and waved a hand at the Prince. "Tell her the story, Far. I'm too tired to give it justice."

Prince Farlis nodded, looking at Andoni with a little worry. "Five years ago, right before the Animal Wars started, Andoni came to the castle," Farlis said. "My father had brought him from the north to train as the new head wizard."

"Many people weren't happy about that—local people, who thought one of them should have a chance at the position," my mother said. She handed Andoni a cup. He sniffed at it and then sipped. "I kept most of that from you and your brothers at the time, Lee. Your father and I were up to our necks in trouble, since we backed the Royal choice. Tash'a'call Andoni was—is—an exceptional mage."

No wonder I hadn't recognize the name! I didn't feel nearly as stupid now. Besides, it made a name like <u>Lefreeanna</u> look tame.

"Outside forces were trying to disrupt the succession to the throne, and Andoni stood as a deterrent to their plans. They kept trying to throw new problems at him, to make him fail, but he didn't," Prince Farlis said.

Andoni shrugged.

"The Animal Wars started because these fools banded together against him, and the spell backfired and spread out over the country. Andoni tried to get it under control at the Battle of Frog Pond. When Andoni realized he was about to be captured, and that I would be in danger with him gone, he did a very tricky bit of magic—"

"Frogs-to-Princes. That hid you in the mass of them, didn't it?" I said.

"Exactly. Andoni disappeared from the battle, and until he turned up here at the castle earlier today, I thought they'd killed him."

"What about the book?" I said, waving a hand toward it.

"My spell book," Andoni said and patted it again. I thought the book snuggled in a little closer, happy for the attention. "I wrote in it for years—little snippets of stuff, including that rather ill-thought spell that brought you to me. The last thing I wrote was my account of the Battle of Frog Pond, right after the encounter, while I hid in the swamp, trying to evade the enemy. I knew they were going to capture me soon. I dropped the book in the weeds. I don't know how long it took to get back to the city, but by then it knew I needed help. Where did you find it?"

"It found me at the library."

"Very smart book," Farlis said. "Andoni says that you were very brave, Dove."

Surprisingly, I didn't blush this time, even with my mother right there. "I wanted—well, I'm just glad it all worked out."

"Time for you to rest, Mage," my mother said. "And for me to take my daughter home."

"Oh, of course!" Andoni said. He looked upset. As I started to stand, he caught my hand, wounded fingers tightening around mine. "Dove, you will come back, won't you?"

"You're a fool, Andoni," I said. Then I lifted the hand and gently kissed his fingers. He blushed this time. "*I wish that my own true love would come to me on the wings of a dove.* Of course I'll come back. That spell never would have worked, if I hadn't been the right one."

He smiled, Farlis laughed, and I began to wonder if I could get access to the castle library. I'd heard they had the complete *Chronicles of the Rabbit Rout* somewhere in there...

About the Author:

Lazette Gifford is the Assistant Site Host for Holly Lisle's Forward Motion and Managing Editor of Vision, Forward Motion's ezine for writers. She has published over fifty stories and novels since her first sale in July, 1999. Her works have appeared in over fifteen ezines and three epublishers, with several more pieces waiting to spring at unsuspecting readers. An advocate for Internet publications as a new medium for storytellers, Lazette believes that, short of the fall of civilization, epublishing is not going to go away.

lazettegifford@echelonpress.com
http://lazette.net

Lazette Gifford

What Every Pharoah

Lynn David Hebert

What Every Pharaoh Needs

Carson Jones loved his work at ICRAC: the Institute of Chronomigrant Research in Ancient Cultures. (Originally, it was 'Ancient Peoples,' until they worked out the acronym.) So he was crushed when his boss called him in to tell him the bad news.

"It was either we that got the funding, or that horse racing museum and theme park in Kentucky. Pork barrel politics and political payback won this round. Unfortunately, we have to cut back."

Carson braced himself for the inevitable. As junior scientist, he would be first to go. Also, his probes reached the deepest into the past, and cost the most. Rotten timing, he thought, with his wedding just four months away. His mind drifted off through the repercussions. It was a good thing he hadn't closed on that town house yet. The director raised his voice and broke his chain of thought.

"Did you hear me? You're junior man, and your work is most expensive, so I have to cut your budget. Nothing deeper than four thousand years or so."

"Then you're not firing me?"

"Not yet. You're the best deep probe man I've got. I'm just holding you back until funding improves. But if we get another setback like this Kentucky thing, well..." The chairman shrugged.

Carson scratched his head and frowned. "Kentucky. Isn't that where they kicked evolution out of the high schools?"

"Someplace out there. So?"

"Maybe we're getting too good at time travel. Last month we sent a probe back to 6027 BCE. I'll bet there's some that are afraid of what we'll find if we go back any farther."

"Well, they've got no worry now. Our new budget will keep us pretty close to home: Greece, Egypt, Babylon—"

Carson snapped his fingers. "Fund Raising! Rich folks pay a mint to ride the space shuttle and look back at Earth. What do you think they'd pay to go back and see a real Roman orgy, and maybe even join in on the fun?"

The chairman thought for a minute, and then shook his head. "No good. Half of congress would want to freeload and go on fact-finding junkets. We'd never make any money or get any research done."

A long silence followed, then Carson spoke again. "What if we make our money at the other end?"

"How?"

"The Dutch bought Manhattan for a bucket of beads, didn't they?"

"Only because the tribe they bought it from didn't own it. What's your point?"

"I'll go to Egypt and pick some impulsive teen-age pharaoh who's used to getting everything he wants, and has all the gold in Egypt to pay for his whims. And I'll sell him things that no one back then has even dreamed of. To hell with congress. Were running on the pharaoh fund."

"That's fine in theory, but remember, we can't contaminate the past."

"No problem, at least not with the things I'll be toting back there. Think about it. What if an archaeologist excavates an

Egyptian tomb and finds the remains of television set. Is he going to announce the revolutionary discovery that ancient Egyptians watched television?"

"He's still going to wonder how it got there."

"More likely he'll just look all his workers in the eye and say 'Okay, who's the joker?' But not to worry; here's what I'll do: Whatever I sell will break down or go dead eventually. I'll take it back for repairs, and never return it. Gold and goods both wind up in the present. No contamination."

"It doesn't sound very honest."

"Hey, it's for a good cause. Besides, the pharaoh will have a lot of fun for a while, and let's face it, the guy can afford it."

"Okay, Carson. You're in charge. Don't let us down."

"Like I said, don't worry."

But Carson soon had reason to worry. Being a time-traveling salesman was tougher than he had thought, and more dangerous. As an archaeologist and anthropologist, Carson could study his subjects from a distance in the safety of his time machine. With it's cloaking device he could hover a mile in the air by day and appear as a drifting cloud from below. Any Egyptian seeing a lone cloud in the sky might think it odd, if they thought about it at all. But no ancient mind could ever imagine that the cloud was observing them with powerful lenses and sensitive microphones.

As a salesman, however, he would have to come down and enter society. Although he had studied the Egyptian language, he could never pass as a native speaker, so he had to play the role of a foreigner. But what nationality?

Every land friendly to Egypt sent ambassadors to Pharaoh's court, and merchants and travelers to the rich and wondrous Nile valley. Even enemy nations contributed slaves, some of whom played important roles in court. If anyone tried to talk with him in his supposed native tongue, what could he do—respond in English?

And there he had it. So obvious. A merchant selling goods that no one has ever seen before should come from a mysterious land and speak an unknown tongue. And his clothes? Something cheap and gaudy that would seem rare in ancient Egypt. At a costume shop he bought a sequin covered jump suit and threw away the Elvis wig and sideburns that came with it.

Carson Jones went on down to Egypt in an outfit even Solomon would envy, and he carried with him a thing he knew no teenager could ever resist.

Carson landed by night at the outskirts of Thebes. He set his time machine on autopilot, and with his remote sent it into the air to hover. Since remotes can lose themselves, or break, and such a catastrophe could leave him stranded, he programmed the machine to land again in 24 hours.

He followed the road to Thebes by starlight, laid by until daybreak, and then approached the city gates as a traveler, with a walking stick in his hand and a pack on his back.

The guards must have seen his sequined suit glittering in the morning sun at a good distance and spread the word. When he reached the gate, Maya, the pharaoh's treasurer, waited to greet him. "I have never seen anything like this," Maya said, drawing his hand over the sequined sleeve of the jump suit. "My guards said a stranger was coming, wearing a cloak of jewels. Strange gems. They seem more like fish scales. Do you always wear such outlandish garb?"

"Well, you're not supposed to examine them closely. When you see me in good light from a distance, especially when I stand in a shaft of light in a darkened room, I'm quite impressive."

"Ah! You are a sorcerer then, or an entertainer."

"Better than that. I'm a trader, and I've brought a rare object from the far west. There is no other like it in all the world."

"And what is this object?"

"I've got it in my pack here." Carson slipped out of his pack, lowered it to the ground, and began to open it. "It's hard to explain. You have to see it in action to understand."

"Good." Maya pushed Carson's hand away from the pack's bindings. "The pharaoh loves new and strange things, and he should be the first to see it. Come to the palace at sundown. If you please him you may leave a wealthy man.... Just out of curiosity, does it have anything to do with fish scales?"

"No."

"Good. You may indeed get rich."

That evening, the mud brick exterior of the palace suggested poverty to Carson, but the gold that gleamed in the antechamber where he waited warmed his salesman's heart. He alone worked this territory, for only the government could afford time travel, and only archaeologists could use the equipment.

"He will see you now," Maya said, leading him into a lofty audience hall before the pharaoh. His jumpsuit sparkled in the flickering sconce-light, and the pharaoh and his court hushed in awe as Carson strode with Maya to the center of the room, and made a deep bow.

"Who are you, who comes to us dressed in starlight?" the pharaoh asked.

Wow, have I ever got these guys impressed, Carson thought. He drew himself up to his full six feet, taller than Maya and most Egyptians by a full head. He used a slow, commanding voice, but unfortunately he could speak in broken Egyptian that made the courtiers snicker and the boy king smile.

So much for a stately entrance, Carson thought.

"I've brought you a rare treasure, your highness." He held up a black and silver stereo.

The pharaoh yawned as he examined it. "It's ugly. I have much more handsome chests to keep my things in."

"It's no common chest, my lord. It's called a 'boom box,' and it carries sounds. Music wherever you go. I open this little door, slip this tape inside, and—"

A handclap interrupted him. "Music!" the pharaoh ordered.

A band of young women entered from a side door. Some carried instruments, and they began to play on drums, cymbals, strings and pipes while they sang in rich harmony. Others danced for the pharaoh.

Carson stood transfixed. The tomb paintings of musicians and dancers had seemed crude to him, so the grace, rhythm and sheer beauty of this performance amazed him.

The pharaoh beamed as he waived the musicians away. "You see, I already have music wherever I go. Whenever I want. And can your boom box dance?"

Carson bowed deeply and backed away. "I'm sorry to have wasted your time. I'll find something better to bring you."

"Wait," the king said, motioning him to stop. "I'm curious. A magician once showed me a wonderful puppet that talked and sang. Let's hear the music of your boom box."

Carson pressed the play button and a drum solo rattled out. The pharaoh smiled and tapped his foot, but when the scream and snarl of heavy metal filled the court he jumped to his feet in horror. The court gasped in unison, and Carson hit the stop button.

"Barbaric!" the pharaoh shouted. "Get that thing out of Egypt. Sell it to the Sea-Peoples."

Carson bowed so deeply he almost lost his balance. "At your command. But I swear to you I meant no offense. This box is from a far-off land where the people admire such sounds."

"I do not admire them. What land loves such strange music?"

What land indeed? Carson thought. He didn't want to say America, over three thousand years in the future, nor did he dare to mention any land the king might know. Best to deal with fable. "Atlantis."

The pharaoh nodded, sat back on his throne and regained his royal serenity. "A land of strange devices and riches. But I thought it sank into the sea long ago."

"Well . . . yes, the main continent of Atlantis did, but a colony of Atlantian culture survives far to the west."

"And all its wonders?"

"Many of them."

"Return that boom box. Scour the treasures of Atlantis and bring me something strange but useful. Please me, astound me, and I can promise you a great reward."

Carson took his leave and walked under a full moon through the streets of Thebes to the city gates. A captain of the pharaoh's guard accompanied him, for the shadows of the dark city held danger for a richly dressed person who walked alone.

His mind raced. Because he hadn't put enough thought into this venture, he now had to arrange a second trip. He needed more information if he were to make a sale before his funding ran out. "What would you say the pharaoh needs most?" he asked the captain.

The dark-skinned warrior shrugged. "He has whatever he wants. He owns all of Egypt, the richest land in the world. How can you say he needs anything?"

"Well then, where does his heart lie? Of all the treasures in Thebes, which does he love the most?"

"His heart isn't in Thebes. It's there."

Carson looked to where the captain pointed, and saw the moonlit peak of el Qurn, a natural pyramid, which dominated the horizon. But he knew the captain referred to the valley beneath the peak: the Valley of the Kings.

"His tomb. I should have figured."

"But you can't sell him the one thing he wants."

"And that is?"

"A long life. He must live to build a tomb greater than any that's been built before. He will serve only the gods in the next life."

Carson stared at the rugged peak. The pharaohs no longer built pyramids to attract grave robbers. They hid their tombs deep in the limestone strata beneath the desert. To build a tomb, they dug.

"I know what he wants. Tell the guards at the gate to watch for me, and Maya to be ready."

A week later Carson stood with the king's treasurer at the entrance to Tutankhamun's unfinished tomb and watched a dust cloud approach along the desert road.

"Is that the king in front?" he asked Maya.

"Who else? His horses are the strongest, his chariot the fastest."

As the pharaoh careened up the road to the tomb, Carson saw the exhilaration in the young charioteer's face. The horses rumbled to a halt, the king jumped down and strode briskly to meet him. On his raised throne, and in his chariot, the king had towered over him, but he stood only five foot five. Face to face, on level ground, the pharaoh looked up to speak to Carson.

"Where is this wonder that will make my tomb the greatest ever seen?"

Carson led him and his guard by lamplight down to the antechamber of his tomb. "Stand back here and watch what I do to that unfinished room."

Carson pulled a cord and an electric generator purred to life. As he flicked a switch to flood the chamber with light, he heard gasps of awe behind him. A second switch started an air compressor, and Carson picked up a jackhammer. He looked back at the pharaoh and saw astonishment. Now to please him.

"Get ready for a little noise," he shouted. A thunderous din shook the tomb, dust swirled and rock chips flew as he attacked the limestone wall. When a heap of chips had grown at his feet, he shut down the jackhammer and turned to the pharaoh.

"See how easily I shattered . . . " but his voice trailed off, for he spoke to an empty tomb.

Back in the desert sun, he listened humbly to the pharaoh.

"What if that thunder follows me into the afterlife? A tomb is a place of rest, not a thousand-year headache."

"I'm sorry. I only meant to dig quickly."

"Slow and long is just as good. The priests see a full life for me, another thirty years at least. By then my workers will have built me the grandest tomb Egypt has ever seen. And the most serene."

The pharaoh leaped back into his chariot, and his horses chafed and stamped so that he had to draw tightly on the reins to hold them. "If you could bring me something better than I already have I would make you rich. But in all the strange worlds you wander, you will never find anything greater than what I have in my Egypt. Never finer musicians or craftsmen or artists. Never a faster chariot or stronger horses."

He snapped the reins and his steeds leapt into the road. Hooves thundered on hard dirt and workmen dove into ditches as the pharaoh and his guard raced back toward Thebes.

I've got you now, Carson thought. *Next time we meet, little pharaoh, you'll know there are better things beyond your Egypt. Things you never dreamed of.*

Two weeks later Carson and Maya waited at the desert's edge for the pharaoh, who had accepted Carson's challenge to a race.

The king drove his team up to them at an easy canter and he smiled at the vehicle that Carson stood beside. "That's a homely chariot; so squat and heavy. And look at those thick wheels, like a child's pull-toy. You'd need a dozen horses to haul that thing. By the way, where are your steeds?"

"Right here," Carson said, patting the hood of his dune buggy. "Over two hundred horses under there."

The pharaoh grinned. "I like you, Carson. You have such strange notions and devices. Useless, perhaps, but entertaining. Anyone can see that not even a single horse could fit in there. But let's see what your chariot can do. You know the mark we race to?"

"Your treasurer showed me," Carson said as he slid behind the wheel and fastened his seat belt. "Whenever you're ready."

"I'll wait for you there." The king snapped his reins and his chariot tore into the desert.

Carson started his engine and revved it a bit while the pharaoh built up a good lead and Maya laughed. "Do you need a push?" he asked.

Carson shifted into first and rolled slowly into the desert while Maya laughed even louder. By the time Carson had pulled even with the pharaoh he could no longer hear Maya, but he knew he didn't laugh any more.

"Not bad for a kid's pull-toy," he shouted. The king only lashed harder at his straining horses. "See you at the finish line," Carson yelled as he pulled ahead.

Soon Carson sat on the passenger side as an eager boy-king stood on the seat behind the wheel. "I do not understand how you drive this chariot. Where are the reins, and where do I strike with my whip?"

"No reins or whip, your highness. It's steering wheel and accelerator."

"What?"

"Sit down, like me, and I'll show you."

"A pharaoh must stand straight and tall in his chariot. To sit is demeaning."

Carson looked at the stubborn boy who stood on the driver's seat with his arms folded, waiting for a lesson.

"Don't think of this as a chariot, think of it as a throne-on-wheels. It's dignified and proper to sit on a throne." The boy raised an eyebrow. "Besides, if you don't sit, you can't reach the controls, the things you must use to drive it."

That was the clincher. The pharaoh sat, wriggled into the bucket seat, and smiled. "So comfortable. Could you put one of these on my palace throne?"

"Of course. Now pay attention. This is an important safety feature. It's called a seat belt and shoulder harness."

Carson showed him how to pull the straps across and click them in place. "This is the button you push to release them."

The pharaoh immediately pressed the button, and the belts flew off him. "No straps. To sit is bad enough. The pharaoh will not be bound like a prisoner."

"But its for your—"

"No! That's final. What's next?"

"Well, this is a safety helmet." Carson strapped the hard shell on his own head. "It protects your skull if you, uh, fall out of your seat."

The pharaoh looked a Carson, grinned, and then laughed out loud. "You look like a barbarian. When pharaoh sits on his throne, he wears the crown of the two Egypts, or no crown at all. Enough silliness. He waved his hand at the controls before him. "Tell me what all these things are. Teach me how to drive my throne-on-wheels."

The boy learned quickly and by late afternoon he had gotten the feel of it, and was soon driving too fast over the surrounding dunes and riverbanks.

* * *

That evening Carson stood before Pharaoh, anticipating the promised great reward.

Tutankhamun sat casually on his throne, petting his favorite cat, which lay on his lap. "No one in Egypt has ever seen or even heard of such a marvelous chariot. It must be very rare and dear to you."

"It truly is. But since it gives you such pleasure, I will gladly part with it."

"And so it's only right that your reward should be something rare and dear to me. Gold is too common."

The pharaoh motioned to an attendant who fetched the pharaoh's cat and placed it in Carson's arms, along with a small bag that felt heavy for its size.

"She's Maunefer, the rarest and most sacred cat in all Egypt," the king said. "Her favorite toys are in that bundle. Take good care of her." From the quaver in the boy-king's voice Carson knew that he had made a genuine sacrifice, and he could only bow low and mumble his thanks. He wished he could say that common gold would be just fine, but feared it would show unspeakable ingratitude.

"You have been truly blessed," Maya whispered to him as he left the audience hall.

"Yeah, right," Carson answered.

Later that night he sat by the Nile petting his reward. "You're not a bad cat at all, Maunefer, and a royal cat to boot. Wow! It's going to take a lot of gold to give you the life you're used to. A ton of gold. Do you think I should mention it to Maya?" Carson took Maunefer's warm purr to mean "yes."

The next day Carson found Maya by the desert's edge, watching the pharaoh race his dune buggy. The official frowned as the youngster tore across the flats kicking up clouds of dust and sand.

"About the cat—" Carson started to say.

"No. About this wicked chariot," Maya said. "I'm afraid for my pharaoh. What have you given him?"

"I've driven those things for years, and I'm just fine."

"Well…"

"So don't worry about the pharaoh. Maunefer is the one with the problem."

"What do you mean?"

"She is the most sacred cat of all Egypt, right?"

"So?"

"It will be very expensive to keep her properly in Atlantis. I don't have anywhere near that kind of money. I'm wondering if the royal treasury could give Maunefer a stipend?"

"Of course. Whatever she will need. Oh gods! What is that crazy kid doing now?"

Carson shuddered as tires screamed while the overconfident pharaoh invented the power skid.

"He ought to slow down a little," Carson said. "I'm afraid he'll get hurt."

"Pray that he doesn't, for you're the one who will be held responsible. You gave him this demon chariot."

Carson winced as the dune buggy cornered on two wheels and almost rolled over. "Wahoo!" the pharaoh whooped.

"Uh . . . What happens to me if he gets hurt?"

"If you're lucky, they'll just bury you alive in the desert. But if they want to get nasty…"

A piercing screech interrupted Maya, followed by the clank of crumpling metal. Carson gasped as he watched the dune buggy tumble in a dust cloud and come to rest with its wheels turning slowly in the air. He reached into his pocket, pulled out his remote, and called down his time machine.

While he waited for rescue, he watched the pharaoh's guards pull the boy from the wreck and examine him, as he lay unmoving on his back.

Shortly, the captain left the troop and started trotting toward Maya. Carson looked up to see his machine descending toward him, and prayed it would arrive before the captain did.

The captain drew near and spotted Carson, and then shouted back to his men. "There he is, by Maya. Take him." He waited for his men before approaching Carson, and that small delay allowed the time machine to arrive first. As the troop jogged toward him, Carson stepped into his machine and threw the switch.

* * *

Safe at home, Carson sat reading a book on Egyptology while Maunefer tumbled on the carpet with a new plaything. "So you like my catnip mouse better than the toys your pharaoh gave you?" ICRAC had sold Maunefer's Egyptian playthings, solid gold of course, and earned enough to cover expenses. Ahead by one cat, Carson figured.

In the entry for King Tut, he read something he hadn't noticed before. "Bad   news,   Maunefer.   Your   master suffered a wound: a hole in his head. The experts figure he may have been assassinated, or suffered a chariot accident. You think we should tell them what really happened?"

Maunefer sneezed, shaking her head.

"You're right. Besides, who'd ever believe that king Tut was just a wild kid who rolled his dune buggy?"

About the Author:

Lynn David Hebert grew up in the Green Mountains of Vermont, where his favorite pursuits were roaming the fields and woods and reading classic books from the town library. At St. Michael's College he majored in Philosophy, and minored in the Classics and Science. After college he turned to science teaching and earned a doctorate in Science Education from SUNY at Buffalo. Lynn now teaches Science and Computers at several local colleges in the Green Mountains. He has published several stories, some poetry, and a novel.

ldhebert@echelonpress.com
www.chateauhebert.com

Holy Roundness

Kfir Luzzatto

Holy Roundness

"Wake up, Dan! Wake up," yelled the voice that came from the receiver that I had managed to bring to the pillow, next to my ear.

"Wha—?" I mumbled into it.

"Can't you wake up and open the door?" said a familiar voice.

It sounded like my old pal's, Stephan Poulosky, but of course I knew it couldn't be him. I was plainly dreaming. The watch near my bed said it was two o'clock in the morning, and people don't ring people up in the middle of the night, do they?

"Steff?" I asked, playing along with the dream.

"Of course it's Steff, blast you! Get up and open the damn door, will you?"

"Yeah, yeah," I answered, and put the receiver back. My dream-master was slipping, becoming incoherent. As a rule I don't mind a weird dream every now and then, but I make it a condition that it has to make some sort of sense, and this one didn't. The person in a proper dream had to be either on the phone or at the door, not both.

I decided to beat the dream and go back to sleep. But something got in the way. It was the door. Someone kicking it and the racket it was making threatened to wake up the whole building. So perhaps it wasn't a dream, after all.

I got up and hurried over. When I opened the door I got a nasty shock. The first thing I saw was a beard. When I say 'a beard,' one shouldn't get the impression that what presented itself to my view was a decent beard, such as worn by regular people. It was nothing of the sort; the outgrowth was so long and bushy that it obscured everything else. Not something to spring on you without warning in the middle of the night.

At first, I averted my gaze from the excrescence, but then I forced myself to look again. Further inspection revealed that old Steff was buried behind it. I hadn't seen him in five years, but I would have recognized him anywhere. He was holding a cellular phone in one hand, which accounted for it all.

Steff and I had met at the university where I was studying physics and he was working toward a master's degree in philosophy. We had seen a lot of each other for three years, but then I had left to get a proper job, while he kept his endless studies on, and we had lost touch with each other. I had heard that he had got religion, though, but I never got around to tracking him down to see what had become of him.

Now I saw it, and it wasn't a pretty sight. He was wearing a black robe and had put on a lot of weight. His headgear, also black, looked like a chef's hat, but was round at the top. The esthetic composition took my breath away. I stood there, gaping at him, unable to find something to say.

"Well," said Steff, testily, "are you going to let me in, or do I have to go on kicking the door?"

"No, no, I'm sorry, come in," I said, moving to one side.

I closed the door and we went into my small living room, where Steff sat himself heavily on the sofa and took his face into his hands. I looked at him, debating with myself whether I couldn't simply leave him there and go back to sleep. He looked as if he wasn't planning to emerge from his lethargic state for a while anyway; but on the other hand, simply ignoring him was not in line with my duties as a host. Resigned, I addressed him.

"I need coffee," I said. "Do you want some?"

"I could use something a bit stronger, if you don't mind," mumbled Steff, through his fingers.

I nodded—wasted on him, of course, since he wasn't looking—and went to fix drinks. Five minutes later I was back with a cup of coffee and a glass of scotch that I put on the tea table beside him. I sat in an armchair in front of him, sipped my coffee and started to feel human again. Steff lifted the glass and drank most of it in a single gulp, then sat straight up and looked at me. I noticed that his beard was quivering, and I could swear that he was praying, or something.

"Well... it's been a long time," I said, feeling that the conversation was languishing a bit.

"I'm in a fix, Dan," said Steff, ignoring my remark and looking over my left shoulder with glassy eyes.

"Tell me all about it. I hear that you have become some kind of priest..."

"Yes. I am a minister of the Temple of the Holy Roundness. You, of course, being a soulless individual, don't have a clue, right?"

"I don't think that 'soulless' is called for. I may not be very religious, but…"

"What do you know about the Holy Roundness?" he interrupted.

"Well, you know, life being so busy..."

"Then I'll have to explain to you," said Steff with a sigh. "The Temple of the Holy Roundness was founded ten years ago by our patriarch, the Reverend Father Sphericus the first, whose name before The Revelation was Mark Shain. The Reverend Father used to sell life insurance and, as a result, spent most of his time traveling and learning the ways of people. He was particularly led to meditation by the callousness of those who, when approached about a perfectly reasonable life insurance plan, where not humble enough to understand that their days on this earth arc numbered. He was much saddened by their constant refusal to purchase life insurance, and their lack of understanding of the cyclic nature of life and death.

"His meditations led him to the understanding that Salvation will come to us through roundness, since all that is perfection is round, and all that is round is perfect. He founded the Temple of the Holy Roundness, but for the first few years he acquired only a small number of followers. Then came the miracle that changed all this..."

I remembered reading something about the sect worshipping something or other, but I couldn't quite recall what it all was about, so I let him go on.

"One day, when the Reverend Father was walking in meditation by the river, the Holy Sphere revealed itself to him. The Holy Sphere," he explained, "is a perfectly round ball of metallic aspect. It is shiny, and it hovers exactly a meter and a half above the ground. It emits a pleasant music at regular intervals. It follows the Reverend Father, wherever he goes..."

"Just like Mary's little lamb," I observed, drawing a nasty look from Steff, who went on, ignoring my remark.

"It follows the Reverend Father, as I said before you interrupted, wherever he goes, unless he orders it to stay in the chapel that houses it."

I suppressed the impulse to remark that this sphere was better housebroken than many dogs, and limited my reaction to an intelligent nod.

"Armed with this undeniable proof of sanctity, the Reverend Father acquired many more followers, and the Temple of the Holy Roundness has now over a million of them. A cathedral was built near the spot where the Holy Sphere was found, and now houses it, and is the seat of power of our faith."

"All this is very interesting," I said, trying to keep myself from dozing off, "but why can't the lecture wait until morning?"

"Because tomorrow morning I will be doomed," said Steff, accompanying the remark with a hollow laugh. "I'm in a fix, I tell you, and I need your help."

"OK," I said, resigned. "Let's hear it."

"As an honor imparted only upon the highest priests of our temple, I was on watch duty tonight. During the watch, which lasts forty-eight hours, the priest stays by the Holy Sphere, eats there, sleeps there, and always keeps his eyes on it. Our presence is ritual but also has the purpose of ensuring that nobody touches the Holy Sphere or otherwise desecrates it. It is our primary duty to make sure that nobody goes near it."

"And…?" I prompted him, failing so far to see the point of the story.

"And we, the priests, are also not supposed to touch it. But tonight…"

He paused and looked away, as if in shame.

"What did you do?" I asked, fearing the worst.

"I…," he began, but his voice broke. He swallowed twice and went on.

"I saw a speck of dust on its surface. It wasn't much, just a tiny little speck, but it drove me mad. It was conspicuous and much as I tried to ignore it, my eyes kept going back to it, like a magnet. So I had to clean it. I took my handkerchief, moistened it and rubbed the Holy Sphere gently with it."

151

"Well, I can see that you feel guilty about it, but it's no big deal. I'm glad that you came to me to unburden your soul. Don't give it another thought, really. Now finish your drink and we can all go back to sleep."

"You haven't heard it, yet," said Steff in a frosty tone.

"I haven't heard what?"

"You haven't heard what happened next."

"Well, then tell me, for Heaven's sake!"

"It…opened up," he whispered.

"It what?" I asked in surprise.

"Opened up! Are you deaf?"

"And what was inside?"

"Well, it's more like a glass sphere with an inner reflecting surface. The upper hemisphere suddenly stopped being reflective and became transparent. And inside…" he stopped, obviously overwhelmed by the recollection of what he had seen, "… inside I saw the figure of a person. A miniature person who looks very alive and moves around.

"You mean to tell me that someone lives inside that sphere?"

"I don't know. I was so scared by what I saw and did, that I just ran away. I locked the door of the cathedral behind me and started to walk aimlessly in the street, trying to figure out what to do. I didn't know whether I should call the Reverend Father, or just go and kill myself in some quiet corner. Then I remembered you and came here. May I get a refill of this," he added, handing me the glass. "I think I need it."

"Yes," I said when I'd refilled the glass and handed it to him, "this is all very well, but what can I do?"

"You are a physicist, aren't you? Then you may be able to find out how to put the Holy Sphere back together again."

"Mm… But why can't it wait until morning? I think much better when I've got some sleep."

"It can't. My shift ends tomorrow morning at six. The priest who will replace me is Brother Chrispine, my worst enemy. Let me tell you about Brother Chrispine. He is a sleaze ball. I strongly suspect that, prior to joining the Temple he sold used cars. I won the Round Verse Poetry Competition that was run by the Reverend Father last month, in spite of the fact that Chrispine spent most of the week before the judging sucking up to him. He came in second, and now hates me for it. If the problem is not solved before his shift begins, he will denounce me to the Reverend Father, and that will be the end of it. I will be thrown out of the temple."

"Perhaps you could go to the Reverend Father," I suggested, "and come clean. It looks to me as if you meant well. I'm sure he will understand and require you to do some trivial penance, like reciting some prayer fifty times, or something."

"You really know nothing about us, do you?" Steff asked with scorn. "Our faith is about perfection, not about mercy, leniency and all that nonsense. The moment I tell the Reverend Father what I've done, I'm history."

"Can't you…"

"No. That's no good either," he said, getting up. "You must come now. We're running out of time."

* * *

The cathedral of the Holy Roundness was an impressive building, with round windows and doors, round seats and round ceiling. Every single part that could be so made, was round.

We were standing at the altar, looking at the Holy Sphere. It was indeed impressive, floating there peacefully, at eye level, the size of a basketball. All was quiet when we got there, but soon a beautiful melody emerged from the sphere. I didn't know what the gadget was, and I strongly suspected that Sphericus the first had found a clever way to fool his followers. Nevertheless, I could see how a simple mind would be taken by it.

"Look here," I said, "before we start on this, we need to have a Plan B."

"What for?"

"In case I won't be able to make it go back to its original shape."

"There can't be a Plan B. If the Holy Sphere stays open, the moment Brother Chrispine walks in he will denounce me to the Reverend Father and I will be blamed. Period."

"You can deny the whole thing. You can say that it changed its shape without any intervention of yours. You can say that you didn't notice. Stout denial. That will do the trick."

"I am surprised and pained by your suggestion, my friend. I am a priest. I could never state but the pure truth. Besides, the prophecy says that the Holy Sphere will stay here to protect us until evil touches it. That is why we keep watch. No, it won't work."

With a heavy heart I turned to the sphere. It looked perfectly uniform and I could see no button or marked area that might signify a key or actuator. Steff had probably touched a pressure button that had activated something inside it, but I couldn't find where it was.

I decided to study the inside of the sphere, searching for a clue. What I saw was really amazing. It looked like a miniature kitchen, and a miniature woman was moving around it, carrying out what seemed to be kitchen chores. She was moving plates and other objects from one receptacle to another, and her apron was clearly visible. The scene was amazingly realistic, highlighted by invisible spotlights coming from nowhere.

I knocked on the glass to see if that would attract the attention of the woman, but if she noticed anything at all, she decided to ignore me. I watched her, almost hypnotized. She had closed the door of what seemed to be a kitchen appliance, and now she pirouetted along the kitchen with uncommon grace. I could swear that she was singing merrily, but no sound filtered through the glass that covered the kitchen.

Along the perimeter of the sphere I could see a legend inscribed in the floor of the kitchen, but much as I tried to read it I could make nothing of it, because of the light. I took out a flashlight that I had thoughtfully brought with me and tried to illuminate the letters, but the light didn't penetrate the sphere. I was baffled.

"Come here. Steff, look at it."

"If you don't mind, I'd rather not," said Steff, looking reluctantly in my direction. "What do you see?"

"Well, I see a kitchen with a woman in it. She looks very real and she's moving in there. Any idea of what this could mean?"

"No. Not at all. Can you close it back?"

"I can't see how. There is no button or instructions, or anything else I can use. I'm sorry."

"A fat lot of help, you are," he said, ungraciously. "I shouldn't have counted on you. So what do we do now?"

"I…"

"Shut up and hide behind a column," he whispered. "Someone's coming."

I hid best as I could, and I could still see Steff, standing there outside the altar.

"The Holy Roundness be with you, Brother Stephan," said a voice coming from someone I couldn't see.

"May the Holy Roundness be with *you*, Brother Chrispine," answered Steff. "You are early."

"When the faith calls," answered Brother Chrispine piously, "time doesn't count. I am eager to begin my service to the Holy Sphere. Anything unusual to report?"

I hazarded a peek and looked at Brother Chrispine. He was blond, thin, and with a short, unimpressive blond beard. He also wore the black costume with the funny hat which, on him, looked even more ridiculous than on Steff's head.

"Well, in fact, I believe that I have been miracled."

"You?" asked Brother Chrispine with scorn. "You wouldn't recognize a miracle if it was served to you on a silver plate. What game are you playing? Wasn't it enough that you managed to mislead the Reverend Father into believing that the round verses that you submitted were not a plagiary? What new lies have you cooked up this time?"

"You surprise and pain me, Brother Chrispine. But in this holy moment, I won't get into a brawl with you. Suffice it to say that the Round Verses that I humbly submitted to the Reverend Father were my own and were inspired solely by my faith in—and love of—the Holy Roundness."

"Tcha!" said Brother Chrispine, derisively.

"Tcha to you, Brother Chrispine," retorted Steff, "with bells on."

"I'll remember that, Brother Stephan," said Brother Chrispine, menacingly, "when the time comes. Now, if you don't mind, I would like to know what is all that nonsense about you having been miracled. And be snappy about it, will you? I am supposed to take over your watch."

"What happened was that I knelt here, in this very spot, deeply absorbed in prayer, when a voice inside me told me to approach the altar. A heavenly music filled the chapel and I, awed by this holy occurrence, got up and approached the Holy Sphere. When I got there I discovered that it was changing."

"In what way?" asked Brother Chrispine.

"It was opening up, showing us the way and bringing us nearer Salvation. No doubt you remember the Prophecy that 'Salvation will come when the Holy Sphere gives the sign.' I believe I have just witnessed the sign."

So much for the 'priest's pure truth,' I thought bitterly. I retreated more deeply behind the altar's columns, to hide from Brother Chrispine's view while he walked swiftly toward the sphere. He stood there for a whole minute, looking at it and checking his watch, and then turned to Steff.

"I believe that you are telling the truth for once—strange as this may seem," he said, at last. "Have you informed the Reverend Father?"

"Not yet."

"Are you aware, Brother Stephan," said Brother Chrispine with a wicked smile, "that the canon requires that any occurrence be brought by the watching priest immediately to the attention of the Reverend Father? You screwed up—sorry, you *misbehaved*—this time. My shift has begun one minute ago, and now it's my duty to inform the Reverend Father. Since you didn't report the event, you are either guilty of gross misbehavior which, I'm happy to say, may cause you to be unfrocked, or we may agree between us that this never happened until I got here."

"Why would you do this for me, Brother Chrispine?" asked Steff, eyeing him narrowly.

"Definitely not for you, my dear friend. It is clear that if the miracle happened during my shift, the credit will be only mine. If I decide to help you out of the spot you've put yourself in, I want no argument about who witnessed the miracle and on whose shift it took place. Understood?"

Steff managed to look sad—although not much expression ever filtered through his beard, and one had to use his imagination to figure it out. "You're right," he said. "I made a stupid mistake and I must now pay for it. I won't challenge your merit in the reporting of this holy event. I will even support your statement that it all happened only when you approached the Holy Sphere at the altar, without any intervention on my part."

"That's my boy," said Brother Chrispine with a satisfied smirk. He turned to the far end of the temple, where he spoke at length into a receiver. Steff approached me stealthily and spoke in a whisper.

"How was it as an improvisation?"

"You did fine. I liked your style. But what about that 'pure truth' you were telling me about?"

"No time for that now," said Steff, waving my question aside. "Get out that way" he said, pointing at a door to one side of the chapel.

"Wait a second," I said, "I want to take a last look at the sphere."

"OK. But be quick about it. The Reverend Father will be here in a matter of minutes and I have no way of explaining your presence. So you can't be caught here with me."

"All right," I whispered back. "Show me the spot that you rubbed."

"It was about here," said Steff, pointing at a spot on the sphere and shivering a bit, and then hurriedly left the altar.

I looked at the spot but could see nothing different from the rest of the surface. I felt it, then pressed it and then started applying a pressure in circles around it. I apparently touched a switch because the sphere started to vibrate slightly. Suddenly, the light inside the scene changed, rendering visible the legend that I had spotted before. Also the pace of the figure working in the kitchen quickened, and the sphere started to glow.

I looked at the main entrance to the temple from which excited voices were coming.   A third priest had arrived. Judging from the amount of gold on his robe and from his majestic demeanor I assumed that he was the Reverend Father. Brother Chrispine was walking backwards, bowing, and I guessed that he was impressing on Sphericus his many merits in bringing about the miracle.

Suddenly the three quickened their pace. They had apparently noticed the light coming from the sphere and were hurrying toward the altar. I retreated behind a column far away from it, near the little door at which Steff had pointed, and watched them reach the altar.

"Praise the Holy Roundness," exclaimed the Reverend Father. "The Holy Sphere is coming to life. The Revelation has begun."

They fell on their knees, watching the changes that were taking place in the sphere. A much louder music was coming from it, and a colorful lights show illuminated the scene in the miniature kitchen.   Something was undoubtedly about to happen.

"We are about to be saved!" said Brother Chrispine, his head bowed in awe.

"The Holy Roundness is revealing itself to us," added Steff. "We are the chosen ones."

"Let us pray, my children," said the Reverend Father, in tears. "This is the moment we all have waited for. Repeat after me..."

I moved toward the door, missing the words of the prayer that the Reverend Father was leading. I didn't mind going away now and missing it. I knew exactly what the sphere was, and where it had come from. It wasn't, as I had suspected, a fraud engineered by Sphericus. Quite the contrary. It was genuine.

I was enough of a physicist to know that no man-made device could defy gravity as that sphere did - and I had examined it very carefully, to exclude all possible tricks, like the use of a magnetic field or of invisible strings. And if the "person" who walked around the kitchen was, as it seemed, a three-dimensional projection, its quality was amazing and required optical capabilities far beyond human resources. My first reaction to it had been that the sphere must have come from another world. Perhaps it was an alien probe - or worse, a weapon.

My relief, when I understood that it had not come from outer space, was therefore immense. Time warping, with which many of my colleagues liked to toy, was a possibility which I had never seriously considered before - but now I saw no other explanation for the events that I was witnessing. Amazing as it seemed, I realized that it had come from the future. I knew this by the inscription that stated: 'Made in Switzerland. © 2030. All rights reserved.'

I also knew exactly what its function was. The legend that I was finally able to read left no doubt about it—the very legend which, I believed, was about to be projected onto the white wall behind the sphere. It said: 'You are about to watch the demonstration of ROUNDY: our new space-saving dishwasher.'

That was what the sphere was about. It was an advertisement, and one had to admit that it had received its fair share of attention.

I tiptoed out quietly. I wasn't in the market.

About the Author:

Kfir Luzzatto was born in Italy, and in 1971 moved to Israel, where he completed his PhD studies in chemical engineering and became a patent attorney. He has published extensively in the professional and general press over the years, totaling more than 160 articles. For almost four years, and until recently, he wrote a weekly "Patents" column in Globes (Israel's financial newspaper). His book on the subject, "The World of Patents", was published in late 2002 by Globes Press. His fiction has appeared in "Fiction Inferno" and in "The Harrow".

kfirluzzatto@echelonpress.com
http://www.kfirluzzatto.com

The Woman Who Couldn't Say No

Janet Miller

The Woman Who Couldn't Say No

"You promised us," he growled. "You promised you would show us the way. Why do you refuse now?" Tall, broad-shouldered, and dressed only in a narrow skirt of leather strips, my very male visitor stood in the middle of my nice suburban kitchen and demanded my help.

My help. As if there was anything I could possibly do for him, or his people. I mean, what could a middle-aged divorced mother of two possibly do for a barbarian chieftain from the twelfth century?

It all began yesterday at Melissa's birthday party. Everyone from the book group was there: Joanna, Alice, Martha, and me. We were doing the things that we usually do when we get together—discussing the latest books, chatting about our kids, drinking iced tea, and eating chocolate cake.

But then Melissa opened her presents and one was a "past-life regression therapy" CD from Alice. Well, of course we had to try it. Melissa turned out to be an Egyptian queen, Martha a slave girl in Calcutta. Alice and Joanna tried it and found nothing, no past lives at all.

Then it was my turn. I closed my eyes, listened to the hypnotic voice on the CD, and found myself drifting back in time. My jeans and sweatshirt disappeared and I felt as if I wore a comfortable, loose-fitting robe. I opened my eyes and glanced at my feet. My Reeboks had turned into leather sandals that tied around my ankles.

I smelled smoke and heard screams. A village of wood and stone surrounded me, flames licking at the straw roofs of some of the huts. Nearby, a child cried for its mother. For a moment I thought it was my little one, then remembered I didn't have any children, it wasn't allowed. I was the wise-woman and forbidden to have a family. For a moment that old sorrow tore at my heart.

Then I heard him, shouting boldly at our attackers. I turned and spied Lord Barron, our village chieftain, on the low battlement surrounding the village. A tall man, he stood with axe raised, defiant against the enemy scattered in the fields below, apparently oblivious to the arrows, some aflame, that sped past him into the village.

Terror for him overcame me, forced me to run to his side. I climbed to the top, calling to him, "Get down, they will hit you." He stared at me, an uncertain look on his face. "Get down," I repeated. "I will show you how to win against them, I promise."

He turned and clasped me in his strong arms, pulling me up onto the wall next to him. An unfamiliar thrill took hold of me at his warm embrace. But then an agonizing pain speared through me. I glanced down to stare at the feathered shaft protruding from my side. *Well, at least it isn't on fire.* I couldn't breathe. He clutched me close to him and I heard my name on his lips. *Eleanor.* The last thing I remembered was the deep velvet blue of his eyes.

Those same eyes now stared at me from across my modern four-burner cook top. I'd just finished shoving the kids out the door and off to school when I heard a noise coming from my kitchen. I'd returned to see a green glow hovering in the middle of the air, a glow that expanded until it filled the room. I shielded my eyes from the light and when it faded, my man from the village stood there, still wielding his axe. At first we just stared at each other, then he'd explained why he'd come.

In this time line, I'm known as the volunteer queen. Anytime someone needs an extra hand at a craft fair, or a bake sale, they call me; I can never say 'no' to a worthy cause. I even keep my hours as a game developer to a minimum so I can help out, although since my divorce I've been reconsidering that. I've needed extra money since Harold left the kids and me. Child-support only goes so far, and I had the credit-card bills to prove it.

Apparently my volunteerism wasn't something restricted to my current life. Once upon a time, I'd been a wise-woman in this man's village, and had promised to help them drive off their attackers—a promise I'd fail to fulfill due to my untimely death. My visitor, Barron, had come to see that I kept that promise.

Death was no longer an excuse.

Just my luck. When the regression therapy CD had been opened at the party, I'd been initially reluctant to try it, figuring that one of my past lives might have had some unfinished business that I'd promised to take care of. It seems I was right and the result was staring me in the face, all glowering six-feet of him. I didn't like the way he held that battle-ax of his, either.

I found my voice at last. "Lord Barron, I'm not refusing to help you. It's just that I'm not sure what I can do."

He narrowed his eyes. "'Eleanor the Wise' we called you in my time. And not without reason, you were the one we could come to when there was trouble and you always had the answer." He studied the floor. "Your loss that day was catastrophic for us."

"It wasn't so good for me, either." Barron glared at me.

My attempt at levity having failed, I gestured for him to continue. "Tell me what happened... after I died."

"We were able to drive the enemy tribe off, but they won't be gone forever. They will soon return and we lost too many men to be able to withstand them again. Before the wizard sent me here, he told me we have but two handfuls of days, no more than ten before they'll attack again."

Barron stared into my eyes and I felt caught in that velvet-blue gaze. "The wizard saw you run to me and watched your spirit when it fled at your death. He used his magic to track it here and found the incantation to send me to this new life of yours." One hand grabbed both of mine in a firm grip and I struggled against the familiar thrill of his touch. "You must help us, Eleanor, we need you sorely."

I felt the word 'no' form on the tip of my tongue, then slide off as it had so many times before. Reluctantly I nodded my head. "All right, Barron, I'll see what I can do."

He smiled at me and released my hands. The smile threw my heart into loop-de-loops—I'd always been a sucker for a great smile. But, then, I realized, I'd always been a sucker for this man's smile. "Just don't expect much. Helping out with a garage sale is one thing—saving an undermanned village with twelfth century weapons and barricades..."

Suddenly I had an idea and my heart began to race. Leaving Barron behind, I raced to the family room where my home "office" is located. Hurrying to my desk, I started up my computer. The machine whirled to life, the screen blinked twice, and the happy face icon winked at me.

"What is a 'garage sale'?" I heard Barron enter behind me, then his gasp as he saw my computer screen change to my favorite shade of blue and the little program icons dance around the screen. He pointed to the monitor with his axe.

"What sorcery is this?"

"Um, well..." I struggled for the words to explain my early twenty-first century technology. "It's a kind of magic box. I can use it to predict what will happen to the village."

Magic was something Barron felt comfortable with. He nodded wisely and settled onto the worn leather couch as I brought up my simulation program.

My game-programming specialty is battle modeling. I'd often wondered why I was so interested in fighting with ancient weapons—maybe it was all that past-life experience impinging on my present.

As the simulation design program came up on the screen, I gestured to Barron to pull up a kitchen chair next to me. "To make this work, I'm going need all the information you can give me about the village and the other tribe. I'm afraid my memory of the place isn't good enough."

It took all morning and half the afternoon, but Barron and I recreated the village and surrounding countryside, then modeled the army attacking them. I showed him how he could add defensive barricades to the fields around the village, describing what they were made of while we worked. His eyes glowed as he began to comprehend my strategy, to keep the enemy trapped in certain areas so that a few defenders would be the most effective. We came up with a plan, one that would require a few days to create barricades. I set up the simulator to run through the plan with different sets of parameters on the attack side, to verify that it would work, and started it.

The simulation would need a couple of hours to run and I decided that Barron should stay until it finished. I found a bag in the garage destined for charity, and pulled out some of my husband's old things, a pair of jeans he'd gotten too heavy for and a stretched out sweatshirt that almost fit across Barron's broad shoulders. I figured I could introduce him as a fellow game designer to the kids. It would help explain his uncut hair and beard, as well as his odd mannerisms.

Barron was a pretty good sport about my insistence that he clean up and change clothes before the kids got home. I took him into the bathroom and showed him how to use the shower and the rest of the facilities. He loved the hot running water and hair dryer, although he refused to use my shampoo, saying it smelled too much of flowers.

The toilet particularly fascinated him. He must have flushed it more times than my kids did when they were two-year-olds.

My son, Kyle, is fifteen and my daughter, Jenny, twelve. Both are good kids, if a bit mouthy. Neither expected to see Barron when they got home.

I introduced him and for once, Kyle's manners were good, probably due to the chieftain's size. Even in ordinary clothes and without his ax, the chieftain was impressive. Kyle actually shook Barron's hand. When an uncomfortable silence descended on the room, I suggested the kids get to work on their homework.

"But Mom, it's Friday, we have the whole weekend!" Kyle protested.

"Well, then…" I fumbled around. I didn't need them asking Barron too many questions. "Maybe you could watch TV for a while. You can use my bedroom," I added, offering that forbidden treat as a way to keep them out of the family room.

They ran off while Barron watched, a wistful smile on his face. I fixed a quick dinner for the four of us, fried chicken, and cut-up vegetables, so Barron wouldn't have to use silverware. He seated himself at the breakfast bar that faced across the cook top and tentatively took the bottle of beer I offered from the refrigerator. It wasn't much to his taste; he made a face and put it down after one sip.

The bottle was one left over from my dearly divorced husband. Harold had never had good taste, in beer or in women. Except me, of course, but now I was no longer to his liking. I'd gotten too old for him, he'd told me during our last fight, before he'd taken off with his latest floozy. At forty I'd become too old.

Barron watched me cook, a quiet look on his face. "I'm glad to see that in this life you have children, Eleanor."

I nodded as I remembered what I'd learned during my regression. "I guess I wasn't allowed to—before."

He grimaced and glared at his beer. "No. You could not take a man or have children." His strong fingers peeled at the label on the bottle. "A stupid law."

My memory of the past had so many holes in it. "You have children, don't you?"

He took another swig and winced at the taste. "Of course." He shrugged. "A man takes a woman to satisfy his body and sometimes a child results."

It was too much like something my husband would have said. "To satisfy his body?" I said caustically. "Is that all it means to you?"

Impatiently he shoved the bottle away. "That is all it could ever mean to me, satisfaction for the body, not the soul. To satisfy the soul, it can't be any woman, it must be the right one." His voice was a low murmur. He raised his gaze and I was again caught in his powerful stare.

The chicken spattered and I returned my attention to it, ignoring the odd pang I felt at the sadness in his voice. What was it to me that Barron hadn't found his soul mate in the past?

When the chicken was done, I set the table for the four of us. While we ate, the kids told me about their day. Jenny reminded me that I had volunteered to bring a covered dish to a potluck for the teacher's banquet next week.

Kyle snickered. "Mom, you are such a push-over." He glanced at Barron. "They call her 'the woman who can't say no' at school."

Barron scowled. "Why do you say that, as if it were something bad? Are you not proud of your mother, of how much she wants to help other people?" His hand came to rest on mine. "I have known your mother a long time, and she has always been this way, forever thinking of others before herself. That is a wonderful thing, young Kyle. More people should be like your mother; it would be a better world then."

I felt my cheeks flood with color at his words. It had been so long since anyone had told me how much my help was appreciated. His hand on mine also reminded of how I'd missed the touch of a man. Barron's warm regard made me long for more.

Both Kyle and Jenny stared sheepishly at me. "I'm sorry, Mom," Kyle told me. "Everyone knows how much you do. I didn't mean to make fun of it."

I nodded. "It's okay, Kyle." I pulled my hand from Barron's and noticed the look of melancholy that crossed his face. At a loss for what else to say, I picked the obvious. "You guys should clean-up the kitchen." For once their answering groans sounded half-hearted. Maybe some of Barron's words had seeped in.

While the kids cleared the table and argued over who was going to dry, I checked my computer. The simulation had run to the end and the results were very promising. There was a ninety-five percent probability that should the defenses be placed appropriately, the villagers would prevail over their attackers. In some scenarios the results would be even better; the attacking army would be virtually wiped out.

I spent the rest of the evening going over the plan with Barron, making sure he understood it. For a man with a twelfth century education, he was very bright, and picked up on my instructions quickly. We searched through my reference books, and the Internet, for sample fortifications common to the century he came from, and made diagrams of simple-to-construct barriers for him to take back.

Soon it was time for him to go. We waited until the kids were in bed, so they wouldn't see his colorful exit. Barron changed back into his leather skirt while I dragged his axe out from behind the washer in the laundry room, where I'd hidden it from the kids.

Barron took it from me and placed it in the sling on his back. "Thank you, Eleanor, for your help." He took a long last look around my kitchen. "It has been good to see you again. I'm glad to see that this life has been better for you than your old one. Here you have love and a family to take care of."

Sorrow gripped me. "Not love, I'm afraid. At least not anymore. My husband and I..." My voice trailed off.

His eyes narrowed in concern. "Your man is dead?"

"My man does not want me anymore," I told him bitterly. "He says I'm too old a woman for love." Angry at myself for admitting so much, I turned from him.

"If he said that, then your husband is a fool!" He caught me by the arm and pulled me close to him. I caught the fine lines around his eyes, the small signs of aging in his face. "You are no older than I, Eleanor. In our time, you were forbidden to me, but even so, I noticed you." One hand slid down my cheek and cupped my chin. "The day you died in my arms I regretted much. Much more than the loss of a wise-woman, I regretted..."

His voice trailed off as he stared into my face. I realized why I'd felt such fear for him during my regression. It was fear for a man I cared about but could never have. Fear for a man I loved. "What did you regret, Barron?"

A slight smile touched his mouth. "This." His lips dipped to meet mine and a burning kiss passed between us. His hands slid down my back and his warmth and strength seeped into me, filling me with a want I'd not experienced in a long time. "Oh, Eleanor, would that we had more time, I would show you how I feel."

He released me and stepped away. "Alas, that I can't. I must return, now. To stay longer would jeopardize everything. I have my responsibilities, even as you have yours." I could feel his anguish, even as I found pride in how my man from the past kept true to his promise. And now, I'd managed to keep mine to him, to help the village after all this time.

From a bag on his belt, Barron pulled a small round crystal and blew on it. It glowed a brilliant green. In its depths I saw a face, familiar to me, with a long white beard. Through the tears that threatened, I managed a smile. "Tell Krandall I said hello."

Barron laughed that I'd remembered the wizard's name. "I will. Take care, o' Wise One. Do things for yourself sometimes, so others appreciate you more." He grew serious again. "One more thing: open your eyes. You take it too much for granted that your age is important. Many men would desire one such as you." He almost smiled. "Indeed, perhaps my own soul will show up someday to claim you."

The glow expanded from the crystal ball and filled the room. I shielded my eyes from the glare and in the bright center

I saw him wave farewell. The glow contracted until it was a single point of light, then winked out of existence.

Goodbye, my love. Misery overwhelmed me. I took myself off to bed, had a good cry, and fell asleep.

When I woke, I heard the kids arguing. In no mood for their bickering, I threw on my robe and marched into the family room. "What has gotten you two so riled up this morning?"

"Kyle won't let me play the new game." My daughter glared at her brother, monopolizing the mouse on the computer.

"What new game?" Confused I rubbed my eyes. I hadn't gotten a new game in weeks.

"This one, Mom. It's great!" Kyle was so enchanted by the program that his usual rebel-without-a-clue nonchalance was completely missing.

I peered at the screen. "That's not a game..." My voice trailed off. In my despair last night, I'd forgotten to turn off the computer. Kyle was playing with my village simulation, changing the parameters to improve the defenses.

Jenny watched carefully. "You should put another archer there." She pointed to the screen. "It will help defend along this road." Kyle stared where she pointed, and nodded. He added the additional man.

I watched, amazed. Jenny rarely wanted to play computer games; they were too violent for her tastes. Normally, she'd never battle her brother over the computer, or attempt to play with him.

But this one was different. It was a defensive game where the object was to avoid violence. My simulation could be the 'Holy Grail' of the gaming industry, a strategy game that appealed to preteen girls and teen-age boys.

Jenny turned to me, her voice eager. "Mom, could I invite

Sally over? She could bring her computer and we could play on that."

"Yeah, Mom," Kyle broke in. "Carl could bring his, too. He'd love this!"

Thinking quickly, I agreed. Within a couple of hours, we had three more computers from the kid's friends and soon had two teams testing the game out, Jenny's friends and Kyle's, each battling for the best score.

All day I was kept busy, designing new village scenarios until two of the older boys watched and asked to help. They decided the planning looked like even more fun than the rest of the game. After that, I added a designer module, so the kids could create their own villages. By Sunday night I was convinced I had a hit on my hands.

To make a long story short, I ended up licensing "Village Defender" to my company, Warcrest Games, for enough money to wipe out my credit-card debt once and for all. I was even able to put away enough for both kids' college education, at an in-state school, at least.

The game was voted 'most popular new game of the year' by Gamers Unlimited and became a best seller at Christmas time. Warcrest gave me a huge bonus and promoted me to head designer for their new "cross-market" game division.

Of course, I insisted on staying part-time, so I could still volunteer at the kids' school. The company was so pleased with me, they didn't quibble a bit, just assigned another designer to work with me. The day of the big PTA Bake Sale, he called to discuss our new project. I was up to my elbows in cookie dough, so he agreed to come to my house.

I'd just started to take out the last batch of snickerdoodles when the doorbell rang. Flustered, I ran to the door and opened it. I got a glimpse of a tall, broad-shouldered man silhouetted in the doorway. A deep voice said, "I'm Barry Burton, I think you're expecting me?" He stuck out a hand. I grabbed it with mine, still encased in the oven mitt, and shook once.

"Eleanor Thompson." Too worried about scorched cookies for niceties, I gestured to him. "Come in, I'm just getting something out of the oven." I ran back to the kitchen, not even noticing that he'd followed me.

I got the last of the cookies off the sheets and onto the cooling racks before I remembered my visitor. I turned to find he'd settled himself at the breakfast bar and was watching me, amusement dancing in his eyes. He was a handsome man, his face clean-shaven. Short black hair curled gently around his ears.

He wasn't young. Fine lines gathered in the corners of his face, all the more evident as he shook in silent laughter. But the color of his eyes was velvet-blue. Barron's eyes.

The cookie sheet nearly slipped from my hands. Awkwardly I caught it and placed it onto the counter. A brief look of recognition crossed his face and his gaze grew warm. "Have we met before? I feel like I know you."

I shook my head, then remembered why his name was so familiar. "Barry Burton. Didn't you design 'Medieval Empire'? You're one of the top designers at Warcrest, practically a legend in the company. I thought you'd retired."

He cocked his head and smiled. "I had, but I decided to come back to work after I saw your game. I loved the premise. Besides—" A look of uncertainty crossed his face. "I know this sounds crazy, but there was something about the village that seemed familiar. It was like I could picture it as more than what was on the screen, as if I could imagine the streets and houses, almost like I'd been there before." One hand rubbed the back of his neck. "You wouldn't know why that is, would you?"

What could I tell him, that he was the reincarnation of the chief of that village, the man I'd loved so many centuries before? He'd think me a lunatic and that was the last thing I wanted.

Fortunately, I had a different answer. "Have you ever been to 'Barronsville'? It's a little village outside London that's managed to survive from the twelfth century to today without too many changes. My simulation was based on that."

I'd been amazed when I looked it up on the Internet the day Barron left. Barronsville had survived, thanks in part to me.

That piqued his interest. "Really? I'll have to go there sometime. Hmm, maybe we could even justify it to the company as a business trip." Barry grinned knowingly at me. "The important thing is that we're going to work together on this next project. I hope you don't mind that I asked to help you out?"

"No, not at all," I was quick to reassure him. "I'm looking forward to it."

He smiled. "Good. I was thinking, if you weren't busy; maybe we could have dinner tonight and discuss it more?"

For a moment my heart raced, then I remembered the bake sale. "Tonight, no, I can't."

"I'm sorry." Barry looked chastised. He glanced around the room, noticed the school art-projects on the walls, my son's jacket left lying on the couch – the obvious signs of a family. "I should have realized, you're a married woman…"

"Oh, I'm not married," I told him. "Not anymore."

His smile brightened and the look in his eyes warmed. "Usually, I say I'm sorry when I hear that, but this time I'm not." Barry's grin reminded me of what sucker I was for a good smile.

A blush overtook my face. "You see, tonight is the bake sale..." My voice trailed off as I stared into his eyes. What had Barron said, that I should look to my own interests? I took a deep breath. "On the other hand, I could just drop the cookies off at the school."

His eyes lit up. "Then we have a date?"

Of course I said yes. After all, I can't say no.

About the Author:

Janet Miller has been making up stories for as long as she can remember. In the past few years she's taken to writing them down, committing to ink and paper the characters that previously lived only in her head. When she isn't writing, or taking care of her family, she's a software engineer in the Silicon Valley

janetmiller@echelonpress.com
http://www.millerclan.com/janetmiller

Don't Look Up

Candace Sams

Don't Look Up

"Unit two-sixty?"

"Two-sixty, go ahead."

"See the woman at 3215 Pine Crest. Caller is complaining about noise."

"Roger that, dispatch. Responding from Main and First Streets." Barry put the microphone down, stopped at the stop sign and glanced at his partner of two years. "Guess who?"

"It's three o'clock in the morning. Doesn't she ever sleep?" Lynn asked as she glanced at her wrist watch. "You know what this is gonna be about, don't you? It's about us working radar again. It's the same thing over and over. Why doesn't the Sergeant tell the dispatcher to talk that woman out of calling us three and four times a month?"

"I know, I know," Barry replied and nodded. "But you've gotta admit. It's a slow night. It's not like we're doing much."

"Fine. But we could get a call about those drug dealers driving through here any time now. They're supposed to be in the area according to the guys over at the D.E.A. And what are we doing? Babysitting some old woman who keeps complaining about us running radar."

Barry slowly pulled away from the stop sign and shook his head. "She's old and lonely. But for the grace of God..."

"Yeah, I know. Let's just get this over with. If those drug dealers show up, I want a chance at that bust. Kelly and Filbert aren't going to get another major arrest this month. This one is ours."

Barry grinned. Lynn loved to stay ahead of the only other patrol team that came close to their arrest record. So far, Lynn and he were the top cops in the area and she wanted to keep it that way. But a call was a call and they were the closest unit in the area. Old Mrs. Harper had heard something again so they had to check it out. Who knew? Maybe this time it could be for real.

Five minutes later, Barry pulled their patrol car up a few houses away from Mrs. Harper's neat little cottage. The front porch light was on and they could have pulled up right in front of the place. Following long-standing procedure and common sense, however, they never did so. It was just a safety precaution and one he and Lynn had always followed.

"Okay, you're the contact officer. I had to do this last time," Lynn complained.

Barry smiled. For all her harshness and bluster, Lynn was really a sweetheart. She treated Mrs. Harper like a favorite aunt and always had. He believed part of Lynn's gruff attitude came from being on the street so long, and part of it was because she really liked the old woman and didn't want to admit it.

They walked slowly up the street, glancing around the area and listening for any sounds that might give Mrs. Harper a valid reason to complain about noise.

"Can't hear anything."

"Me either," Lynn agreed. She frowned, shook her head and walked determinedly ahead of Barry toward Mrs. Harper's front porch. Before she knocked on the door, however, she made sure Barry was standing to one side of it just as she was. Cops in any city didn't stay alive by giving folks easy targets. No matter who was calling, procedure was procedure.

Lynn lightly rapped on the door. "Mrs. Harper? It's Officer Peters and Officer Andrews."

The door opened just a crack.

Barry glanced at Lynn, moved in front of the door so Mrs. Harper could see him, and tipped his hat. "It's Barry Peters and Lynn Andrews, Mrs. Harper. You said you heard something?"

"Oh, thank goodness!" She quickly opened the door and stood to one side to let the police officers into her living room.

Lynn smirked and shot a sarcastic look at Barry when she saw the steaming pot of tea laid out on the living room coffee table along with a plate of double-fudge chocolate chip cookies.

Barry took off his hat and laid it on the back of an overstuffed chair. As usual, the inside of the little cottage was neat and clean. And Mrs. Harper had obviously been expecting the ones she called her *two favorite officers*. "What can we do for you tonight? You told the dispatcher something was bothering you? Some noise?" he asked.

"Won't you sit down?" She waved a hand toward the floral covered sofa. "I'm so glad it's you two. I don't particularly care for that Officer Filbert. He's nice. But he isn't like you two."

Lynn smirked.

Barry grinned and looked at the tray of cookies. "May I?"

"Of course," Mrs. Harper nodded. "I know how you like them."

Lynn shrugged and poured herself a cup of tea. May as well humor her. Like Barry said, she was old and all alone in the world. "Very good," she complimented after sipping some of the tea out of a little demitasse cup.

"I'm so glad you like it, dear. It's Early Grey, you know. I remembered it's your favorite."

Barry shot Lynn a look which dared her to act tough now. It was impossible the way the kind old woman was behaving.

Lynn lowered her head in shame.

"Well, what can we do for you tonight, Mrs. Harper. It's pretty late. Did something wake you up? A noise?" He tried to get back to the reason for their visit.

"Oh, yes. Well...it's your radar again. Every time you turn it on, I hear it. And I get the most dreadful headaches from it."

Lynn picked up a cookie, looked away and tried not to smile. She knew it was going to be the radar again.

Barry cleared his throat and took a sip of tea she poured for him before speaking. "Uh, Mrs. Harper, we've sort of talked about this before, remember? You can't hear radar. Maybe it's something else you're hearing."

"No. It's the radar. You were over on Main Street with your radar on, weren't you?"

Lynn coughed, trying not to choke on her cookie.

"Yeah. We were on Main Street. But how could you know that?"

Mrs. Harper leaned forward and motioned for the two officers to come closer.

Barry glanced at Lynn and they both leaned closer to the woman.

"*They* told me where you were," the older woman whispered.

Lynn stared at Barry for a moment, shook her head and poured herself some more tea.

Barry was beginning to see Lynn's point of view. "Who are *they*?" he quietly asked.

Mrs. Harper giggled, put a hand over her mouth to stifle it, and pointed toward the roof of her house.

Lynn tried not to laugh at the old woman's conspirator-like attitude. She was kind of cute with her white hair neatly pinned up, and her blue floral night gown with matching blue slippers. This was Barry's contact, so she leaned back and let him handle it. The entire call would be something she could talk about in the women's locker room when they got off duty in the morning. She was determined that her partner was going to have to buy hamburgers for a week to keep her mouth shut.

Barry took a deep breath and slowly exhaled. This was a new one. Poor old Mrs. Harper was just getting worse and worse about imagining things. But he had to keep control of himself. He was, after all, a professional. "Okay. Why don't you tell me who *they* are," he cast his eyes toward the roof. "And why *they* are telling you where we're working?"

"Oh, they've been watching out for the both you," Mrs. Harper said and she put a hand on Barry's knee. "They don't want anything happening to either of you. They like you just as much as I do. They're the nicest little people, you know. All green with bright black eyes like little coals in their heads. When I get my headaches, they tell me which police officers are working with their radar and where they are. Then, I call the police department. You come to my house and I get to have some company." . She patted her hair and smiled brightly. "There's a little green woman with them and she especially likes you, young Barry. She thinks you're just the bee's knees."

When Lynn started to snicker, her partner shot her a warning glance.

Barry thought for a moment. How was he going to deal with this? Lynn wasn't going to be any help. She was too busy trying not to laugh, and he could only imagine what she was going to say to everyone back at the station. Then an idea came to him.

"If you stopped getting these headaches, you could get some sleep. Couldn't you Mrs. Harper?"

"I dare say," she nodded in agreement. "While I love having you over, it's enough that *they* keep me up sometimes. But I know they mean no harm. I usually go right back to bed when their visits are over. It's just the headaches from the radars *do* keep me awake, you see. It simply takes me hours to get back to sleep when I get those awful pains."

"Well, I think I can solve your problem."

"You can?"

Barry nodded. "Do you happen to have some aluminum foil?"

"Why, of course. I'll get some for you." Without questioning his need for the foil, Mrs. Harper got up and slowly walked into the kitchen.

"What are you doing?" Lynn softly asked.

"Watch and learn," Barry said and tapped his forehead in acknowledgment of his own genius.

Lynn snorted. "Right. I can't wait to see this."

When Mrs. Harper walked back into the living room with a package of aluminum foil, Barry stood up, unrolled a piece and tore it off. "How many windows do you have, Mrs. Harper?"

She put a hand to her chin. "Well, let me see...there are two in the front of the house. One at each end. One in the bathroom then two more in back. Yes, that's all."

Barry grinned and tore the aluminum foil into small squares. There was one square for each window. "Okay, Mrs. Harper, I'm going to solve your problem with the radar. Then you won't get those pesky headaches and you can get some sleep at night after your little green friends come to visit."

"Oh, really? That would be wonderful. But does that mean you two won't visit anymore?"

Lynn finally spoke up. "Tell you what. We'll come by on...on Thursday mornings after we get off duty. Would that be okay?" She looked at Barry for confirmation and he nodded in agreement.

"Oh, that would be lovely. And sometimes on Sunday for lunch?" Mrs. Harper asked hopefully.

"Sure." Barry smiled warmly at her. "I think we could do that sometimes. Right now, let me get these pieces of foil in your windows and I think that's going to solve your radar problem."

"Huh?" Lynn blurted.

"You know about this, Lynn," Barry said as he sent her a go-along-with-me look. "Foil is reflective and it blocks out radar. All it takes is one little square taped up in each window. I don't know why I didn't remember before."

"Oh, yeah," Lynn quickly agreed. "Foil in the windows. Yeah, that'll do it all right." She rolled her eyes and looked away.

"Oh, I'll get you some tape," Mrs. Harper quickly offered, then left the room in search of her spare roll.

Lynn stood up, pinched the bridge of her nose between her thumb and index finger, and tried very hard not to laugh. "You're a friggin idiot! You know that, don't you?"

"Yeah, well this is going to get us out of being called here several times every month. Just wait and see."

Mrs. Harper returned with the roll of tape and handed it to Barry.

Lynn and Mrs. Harper followed him from room to room while he taped equally divided square pieces of foil in each of the windows. "The shiny side has to be out or it won't work," he advised. "We'll just reflect that nasty radar right back out of the house."

Lynn made a big show of nodding. "Yeah. Shiny side out. That's what the manual says."

When he was finished, Barry led the women back into the living room, returned the foil and tape to Mrs. Harper and picked up his hat. "Well, I think that will have your problem solved, Mrs. Harper. If it doesn't, feel free to call us."

"Oh, I'm sure that will do nicely," she smiled and patted his arm. "You're such a good boy. And you're an angel, my dear." She kissed Lynn on the cheek. "I'll be seeing you both on Thursday morning then?"

"We'll be here," Lynn promised, and hugged the woman before walking toward the door.

After they were on the porch, the elderly woman waved goodbye to them, and they made sure she had her door closed and locked again before leaving.

They were half-way back to the patrol car when Barry glanced at Lynn. She was unusually quiet. "Well, aren't you going to say something?"

"What am I suppose to say? Foil! Jeez!"

"I thought it was pretty ingenious. She's seeing little green men, for cryin' out loud. I mean, it stands to reason that if she isn't all together upstairs, we could talk her into believing foil repels radar. If she really thinks she won't get headaches, she won't. How much do you want to bet this works?"

Lynn held up one hand. "Oh, I believe you. But what happens when those little green men get to be a nuisance, Einstein? She's gonna call you to cure that, too. Then what are you going to do?"

He shrugged. "I'll cross that bridge when I get to it." He glanced back at the cottage. "Poor old thing. It's got to be tough living on your own. No one to talk to."

"Yeah. But what can we do except keep our promise to come see her?"

He nodded. "Let's get back on duty." He paused for a moment so she had to stop walking. "Uh, you're not gonna tell anyone about this, are you?"

Lynn turned around to look at him, walked backwards a few yards and just shot him a wicked smile.

"Lynn?"

She got back in the car and refused to answer.

For the rest of the shift, they took a number of calls so Barry never got to question Lynn about what she'd say to the women in the locker room. In fact, some of the calls were serious enough that the incident with Mrs. Harper wasn't mentioned again. They got off duty that morning without further incident. The next night, however, Barry walked out of the locker room and was ready to begin his shift. The on-duty Sergeant came out of his office and motioned for him to step forward, away from the other officers in the squad room.

Barry walked toward the man and held his breath. The expression on his supervisor's face wasn't all that friendly. But then, he was a Sergeant. They always looked like they'd been sucking on something sour. Barry believed it was probably a requirement that a person had to look that way or they couldn't get promoted. When he stood near the supervisor, the man stared at him for a moment before speaking.

"Get your partner and get in my office," the Sergeant ordered.

Barry swallowed hard and got one of the women going off duty to go get Lynn out of the women's locker room. When

Lynn came out, Barry pulled her aside so the other officers couldn't hear.

"I think we've got a problem."

"What's up?" she asked.

"Sarge wants to see us both in his office."

"Alone?"

Barry nodded.

Lynn glanced at her wristwatch. "We don't even start our shift for ten minutes. That can only mean we screwed up somehow."

"Yeah. But I can't figure out what we were supposed to have done."

"Well, don't keep him waiting. Let's get the butt chewing over with." She grabbed his arm and pushed him toward the Sergeant's office.

They glanced at each other for courage before going into their supervisor's office. When they walked inside, the Sergeant looked up from his paperwork.

"Shut the door," he commanded.

Lynn shut the door and took a deep breath. They really *had* done something wrong or the door wouldn't be shut.

"Okay, Sarge. What did we do?" Barry bravely asked.

The Sergeant got up from his desk, pulled open a file cabinet drawer and jerked out a manual about five inches thick. "This is our Standard Operating Procedure, commonly know to the officers who've read it as the SOP." He paused and watched the two police officers squirm a little before tossing the book on his desk with a loud thud. "Where, in this entire book, do you find any procedure allowing us to tell people to put foil in windows to ward off sounds from radar equipment? I'd really like to know because I seemed to have missed that particular chapter!"

"Uh, that was my idea, Sarge. Don't blame Lynn—Officer Andrews," he quickly corrected. He wondered how the Sergeant had found out about the incident.

The Sergeant crossed his arms over his chest and stared at them both before speaking again. They were his best two cops, but it was sort of fun to watch them sweat a little.

"He's my partner, sir. I'll take the blame, too. I could have said something and didn't. It seemed to make the woman happy."

He arched an eyebrow at them both, then slowly broke into a broad grin. "It did. Very much so. She called this morning and wanted to speak with the Captain. Mrs. Harper gave a glowing account of how you two seemed to have stopped her headaches. Seems she got the best sleep of her life and she credits you two for blocking out all the nasty radar noise from the rest of the patrol cars and airplanes from the local airport. She probably won't be calling the dispatcher so much."

Lynn smiled. "Oh, then we're not in trouble?"

He shook his head. "I didn't say that. Next time you get creative with your work, let me know. I don't want to go into the Captain's office again and try to explain just how foil really does block out non-existent radar noise. Got it?"

Lynn and Barry simultaneously mumbled their apologies and promised to keep him informed about such things in the future.

"All right, you two. Get out of my office and get on duty," he gruffly commanded. Then he tried not to laugh when they rammed into each other while trying to get out of his office fast.

* * *

Several weeks later, Barry pulled the patrol car into the parking lot of the local bank. He parked it and began to fill out some paperwork while Lynn dug through the glove compartment to find a new citation book. Since Lynn hadn't brought up the incident with Mrs. Harper, and everything seemed to be working out where the old lady was concerned, he decided not to mention anything about it.

"Where do you want to eat tonight?" Lynn asked.

"I don't know. Local diner out on the Interstate has a chili special."

Lynn smiled when she found the citation book and quickly stuck it on her metal clip board. "Sounds good to me. But guess whose house we have to drive by to get there?"

"Yeah, I know. Mrs. Harper's place. I thought the Sarge was going to chew us a new orifice over that foil thing."

"Well, everything worked out okay. Mrs. Harper is a lot happier. Especially since we agreed to see her after we're off duty. Seems like that foil idea was pretty clever."

Barry turned in his seat, stared at her and openly grinned. "That's the first time I heard you admit it. I told you that idea would work."

"So, you're a flaming genius." She grinned at him. "Because you're so brilliant, I'll buy chili tonight, okay?"

"You're on," Barry agreed. He started the engine of the patrol car and began the long drive to the Interstate diner. "You know it's sad when you think about it. That poor old lady has been all alone for a long time. The only friends she has is whoever she used to call at the police department and some little green men she made up."

Lynn tilted her head in thought. "Wonder what causes folks to see stuff like that? You think it's a chemical imbalance or something?"

"Don't know. Whatever it is, it sure makes me wonder." He chuckled. "I mean, who believes in that stuff anyway?

Normal people just don't go around seeing weird things in the sky. I don't care what these UFO nuts say, there are no such things."

"I know. Half the people who see that stuff have been smoking something strange. Or you can drink enough cheap hooch and you'll see anything."

"You sound like a woman who knows," Barry joked.

She laughed and waved a hand in dismissal. "Just drive, Captain Jupiter! I don't want to hear about green men or Mrs. Harper anymore. It's bad enough that we just have to drive by her place while we're on duty."

Barry took a short cut to Pine Crest and drove up the long street toward Mrs. Harper's house. They were half-way there when Lynn stuck out her hand and grabbed his arm.

"Barry?"

"Yeah?" He glanced down at the vice-like hold she had on his bicep.

"What's that?"

Barry pulled the patrol car over to the curb and looked where Lynn was pointing with the index finger of her free hand. Way up in the sky, to the northeast, there were a series of three green lights. They were nicely aligned at a sort of an odd angle. Then their colors began to change from green to blue. Then back to green again.

Barry took a deep breath. "Okay. Let's just get a grip here. It's probably something from the airport."

Lynn picked up the radio microphone. "Dispatch, this is two-sixty."

"Go ahead, two-sixty."

"Do me a favor, Ruthy. Call the local airport and ask the air traffic controllers if they've got anything on their radar toward the northeast of town, okay?"

There was a slight pause.

"Sure thing, Lynn. What have you got?"

Lynn glanced at Barry and he was making all kinds of get-off-the-air gestures, slashing his fingers across his throat to get her to shut up. "Uh, nothing, Ruthy. Cancel that."

She quickly put the microphone back in its cradle.

"Are you absolutely crazy?" Barry asked as he rolled his eyes and put his hands over his face.

"We can't be the only people seeing this?" she defended.

"You just had to look up, didn't you? Don't you know cops can't ever see this stuff? Not ever!"

She was about to open her mouth and argue the point but there was a blinding flash of light in the night sky. She looked up again at the same time Barry did.

Right over Mrs. Harper's house were three green balls of lights. Each was about the size of a car tire. They were doing a kind of a figure-eight maneuver around each other before settling into a straight line again. A green beam shot out of each of them and down onto the roof of the old woman's house. Then the beams stopped.

Lynn kept her death-like grip on Barry's arm. "Holy crud!"

Barry watched as Mrs. Harper came out onto the porch, and walked out onto her front lawn. She looked up into the night sky, waved up at the lights then stood there. It appeared she was listening to something or someone.

After only a moment, Mrs. Harper turned and looked down the street. She smiled and animatedly waved at the patrol car and its two occupants.

"Sh-she wants us to come," Lynn whispered in a shaky voice.

"No way!"

"We can't just drive off, Barry. She sees us!"

As they watched, the balls began to slowly drifted down the street toward the patrol car.

"Guess who's coming to dinner?" Barry choked out.

As the three green balls slowly approached, Lynn could see a small body moving around within each. The bodies were as green as the balls carrying them, and their faces had large dark eyes which protruded grotesquely. They waved at her and she sat there, unable to think a single coherent thought.

"Do you see them?" Barry muttered.

"Yeah."

"Let's see how fast this car can move." Barry backed the patrol car up for a distance of about fifty yards. When the back end of it got to the nearest intersection, he quickly pulled the steering wheel to the left, which had the effect of throwing the car into a one-hundred eighty degree spin. "We're so out of here it's not even funny."

"What do we do about Mrs. Harper?" Lynn asked, but didn't turn around to see what might be following or what the woman might be doing.

"Poor old lady my butt! Something tells me she can take car of herself." Barry pushed the accelerator down. The patrol car shot through the intersection and flew down the street. It picked up speed with every second that passed. "Let the Air Force handle this. Remember what Mrs. Harper said? One of those things is a woman and it likes me."

As the patrol car sped into the distance, Mrs. Harper smiled and waved congenially at the three lights chasing the patrol car. "Have fun," she called after them, "but bring them back when you're through playing. Tomorrow is Sunday and I've planned such a splendid lunch for us all."

The End...?

About the Author:

Candace Sams was a police officer for eleven years, worked on an ambulance for eight as a Crew Chief, and is now an author. She graduated from Texas A&M University, was a police officer with the State of Texas, was with the San Diego Police Department, taught for the San Diego County Sheriff's Department and she's the senior woman on the U.S. Kung Fu Team. She's been awarded the Medal of Putien from China and the Statue of Tao for martial arts, and holds several International Martial Arts Titles. She's also an Award Winning author of Fantasy Romance.

candacesams@echelonpress.com
http://www.candacesams.com

Chasing His Own Tale

Marc Vun Kannon

Chasing His Own Tale

Ah, I thought, *The perfect beginning.* And I started typing away at my latest opus.

It was a dark and stormy night.

Before I could type another character, the door pounded under a forceful hand. Before I could even begin to answer, the knocker walked in, a vision in colors. Immediately she said, "Don't write another word!"

"Why not and who the hell are you?!" I shot back, irritated at getting criticisms on my first sentence.

She spread her arms wide, looking nonplussed. As if it were obvious, she said, "I'm your Creative Muse. Don't you recognize me?"

Her hair was a different color, and shorter. Her nose had changed shape, her chin as well, while her eyes were violet. Her wardrobe was completely revamped, and she was six inches taller and approximately half of her previous weight. "Of course I did," I lied. "Get out. Don't even close the door."

"What?" she responded, as if wounded, moving to close the door. "Do you think I'm going to let you put out a load of B-L like that and just—"

"I did it on purpose. This is a comic fantasy."

CM was stunned. "On purpose?" she repeated, "But— you're not a comedian, you don't write—"

"I'm giving it a try. My hero—"

CRASH! WHAM! The door, not even closed, nonetheless crashed open again, and a man of truly heroic proportions, bulging muscles and thighs, shining teeth, flowing hair and all, strode through. "You called?" he boomed, swinging his sword in mighty practice thrusts and parries.

CM jumped behind my desk. I merely rested my head on my hand, the beginnings of a headache coming on. "Hi, Fearless." *Damn. I knew this would happen. One shows up, they all start showing up.* "You're early."

"Not so, good writer," he replied heartily. "You are late."

I placed a hand on my chest in good defensive posture. "Hey, don't blame me," I protested. "My muse here is trying to step all over my dark and stormy night."

That was no help. He looked approvingly at CM and she beamed at him (I wish I knew how he did that). Then he frowned a mighty frown at me. "Good. I hate dark and stormy nights."

"Why?" asked CM, still somewhat flushed from his approving look and standing to give one of her own.

"Mud," Fearless Hero and I replied together. FH shuddered while I explained, "It gets in his sandals."

"Oh." CM settled down. She had no time for wimps.

"But it sets the scene perfectly for his entrance," I continued, trying not to sound like I was whining.

"Yes, my entrance," FH rumbled, posing dramatically. "I'm still waiting for my first line."

"Okay," I said, "I have—"

"My personal favorite—" he spoke right over me "—is 'Have at thee, knave,' although 'Have no fear, fair damsel, I'll rescue you' is good, too." He extended a hand to CM. "And speaking of fair damsels—"

She ignored the hand and him, pointedly looking about my somewhat unkempt little parlor for a place to sit.

I tried again. "Well, it's not—"

"You do have a Damsel in Distress, I hope," FH rumbled expectantly, a little bit stung by CM's rebuff, and I just nodded stupidly, rather than get frowned at again. "Good. For a moment, I was a-feared this was a science fiction story. Do you have any idea how hard it is to say 'launch photon torpedoes' dramatically? Ye gods!" The sword started moving again. "'Engage hyperdrive!' Pfeh! Well, then. Just give me my line, and I'll—"

"Crap." I typed quickly.

His hand stilled. "What mean you, 'crap?' How can you lose a line not yet written?"

"I didn't lose it," I replied. "That's the line: 'Crap.' See? Right there." I pointed at the line I'd just written.

"WHAT?" He had a really mighty bellow.

"It's a comedy," said CM on my behalf. I was too busy watching that sword.

"A comedy?" FH rumbled dangerously, resting the flat of the sword on my shoulder. "And I suppose you want me to take a few pratfalls as well, while howling 'crap' at the top of my lungs?"

It took a while to formulate a coherent reply, my eyes fastened securely to the gleaming length of steel at my neck. "Um, no."

"Mmmm," he growled, slowly pulling the blade, inch by inch, across my shirt. "Well, the moving finger has writ," he observed, philosophically, if ungrammatically. "As I see it, there are three things I can do about this." He pulled out his whetstone, starting using it.

I tried to sound nonchalant, in spite of the soft screeching of stone on metal. "Smite me, surrender resignedly to my will, or struggle manfully to the end?"

"I think not," he replied. "I may sue you (*skreek!*), fire my agent (*skreek!*), or see my union representative (*skreek!*)."

My, how...civilized. "Well, let's not do anything rash." Smiting sounded better and better.

He nodded, putting his sword away without fanfare. "I will go to see my rep."

"Let me help," I offered, quickly, generously. "I can put you on ice for a while, if you like."

He clapped me on the shoulder, nearly knocking me out of the chair with the force of the blow. "You are a good fellow. Yes, do that. Nothing too dangerous, mind. This may take a while."

Oh, heaven forbid. I turned to my word processor, started typing furiously. "Okay, let's see...you're running across the terrain, you're approaching the castle, you're...checking the windows, trying the doors, and...Oops, a trapdoor—"

"Surely I checked for trapdoors," growled a low voice at my back.

"Sure you did," I agreed, making sure that he had. "You checked the whole portico for traps, but the whole portico *was* the trap, and the floor just tipped up, dumping you into—"

"A cistern?" he asked, startling me. He was hanging over my shoulder and whispering (he had a very heroic whisper) into my ear.

"No, a chute," I answered easily. "A long, dark and twisting—Oww, you've struck your head. You wake up, shackled spread-eagle on the wall of a dank and foul-smelling dungeon." I looked up at him. "Good enough?"

"Hmm, yes," he drawled, reading slowly. "Any skeletons? Must have skeletons. Good for atmosphere, without the smell."

I pulled myself forward, hands ready. "Okay, a couple of skeletons, of heroes who couldn't escape, left to tell you of the grisly fate awaiting. How's that?"

"Excellent," he said, nodding briskly, and then, "I will return anon." He left, striding forcefully, as usual.

"So now we wait?" asked CM dubiously, going to close the door.

"Of course not," I replied scornfully. "Now we introduce the villain. Um, no, villainess. How about an Evil Enchantress?" I waited, but nothing happened.

"Ahem. *How about an Evil Enchantress*?"

Still nothing.

"HEY, WITCH!"

"*What?!*" she shrieked, in tones of bending metal. Fortunately, the ladies' locker room is down the hall, but still my ears hurt.

"You're on!"

"I captured him already?!" She sounded incredulous. "Well, put him on ice a minute, I'm still putting my snakes on."

I looked at CM, she looked at me. We shrugged. "Why snakes?" I yelled.

"You mean this isn't a Greek gig?" she asked. "I thought you had a Muse?"

"No, *my* muse."

"Oh, thank God. Those vipers are just Hell on my hair," she responded, relieved. "Let me get a comb."

CM sank back into her chair. "*Now* we wait. At least we stopped her before she started super-gluing the damn things into place. Now *that* takes forever to get out."

"How would *you* know?"

She shrugged. "How do you think I got through school? There was a big demand for Evil Enchantresses back then." She shuddered as fervently as FH had, but moments ago. "You would not believe the crap they expected from me, like just because I was evil, I was some sort of—"

"Lunch?"

"No, tart," she corrected, "Oh, you mean *lunch*. Sure, always, whenever. Who pays?"

I checked my watch. "Me. I ordered a pizza a while back and—" What was that sound? Someone actually rang the doorbell instead of crashing through. Wow, it really worked. I'd never heard it before. "—and speak of the devil…"

The door slammed open before I could get there, narrowly missing my fingers. "Here's your pizza," said the delivery…man, rather gruffly, "Sir."

"Rep?" I couldn't believe it. "Reader's Representative, what are you doing?"

"Paying the bills," he grunted, looking about, placing the pizza box on top of my newly typed pages, and a soda right on the wood of my desk, so it made a ring.. Never one for the social graces, Rep. "They canned me. Well, 'deleted my position,' is how they put it, and me with it. Damned editors playing so high and mighty. 'They can read it for themselves,'" he sneered, in a whiny sort of voice. "Like they know what the public really wants. You wanna know how stupid, ignorant, and selfish the people are, there's an easy way: you talk to someone like me, you'll know soon enough. Damned Editors! What do they know—?"

I waved a hand in front of his face. "Uh, Rep? Okay, here you go." I pressed a bunch of bills into his hand, steering him toward the door. "Good luck."

When the door closed behind him, I dragged a hand dramatically across my brow. "Whew. Remind me to delete that pizza place from my files."

CM nodded vigorously, mouth full of hot cheese. The pizza was pretty good, but not if I had to take RR along with it. It was too bad.

"Hey, Author Guy," EE shrieked from right outside the door. "Which is it, ancient hag—" she held up a bundle of rags "—or seducer of virtuous manhood?" She held up a slinky number that hid nothing.

I knew what I'd rather see her in, but CM was watching me like a hawk. "Um, well—" I trailed off, unsure how to put it.

She appeared in the doorway wearing a body stocking. I knew it. *Damned temptress—* "Well what?" she fumed, "Am I a witch or a bitch?"

Well, if you put it that way— "You're a librarian—"

"WHAT?!" All things considered, I preferred the bellow to the screech.

"—PTA, soccer mom, Save the Earth. You're so squeaky clean it makes my teeth hurt just to think about you." A little payback can be fun. She turns fun colors when she's mad.

She was shaking, steam rising, her fingernails tearing strips in her dress. "But... but...I'm Evil!"

"Well yeah," I replied, taking another slice of pizza. "But there's lots of ways to be Evil. In this one, you're so goody-goody and head-toward-the-Light that you go completely through and out the other side. An 'extremism in defense of liberty' sort of thing."

"You based a comic fantasy character on the GOLDWATER campaign?!!"

Ow. That one hurt even with my hands over my ears. Plus I got cheese in my hair and hair in my cheese. "Well yeah. Why not?" Circular file *that* slice.

She seemed to be having trouble speaking. Perhaps it was the fangs and the drool, or maybe I couldn't hear over the lightning bolts. "I should rip your heart out," she gurgled thickly, talons clenching spasmodically. My chair fell over in a sudden gust of wind, and I decided to stay there. On the floor. Behind the desk. Maybe it was a little too much payback. "I should bake your bones from the inside and scatter your ground-up remains to the winds. I should—"

"You should see your union representative," interceded CM deftly. She's so good to me.

Or maybe not. I'd never met the Evil Archetypes Union rep, but EE's eyes started to glow and she smiled. At least the fangs were mostly gone, although they still looked pretty damn long from where I sat—knelt—cowered. Hey, at least I'm honest.

"Oh yes," she practically purred, a much more terrifying sound. "Yes I should. Write, Author Guy. Give me a good rant, and a smooth exit to plot more villainy. I'll be right back."

Boy was I agreeable. "Sure thing," I gulped, nodding, as I righted my chair and sat down at the keyboard. "You bet. I've got just the thing, magic chains that have a razor-sharp edge no matter how you grip them. Let him try to get out of those, hee hee hee. So long, hero, enjoy the company of your friends as you starve and rot, ha ha ha. I'd love to watch, but I have to go cast my new spell, take over the world to protect it from itself and besides it'll take days of suffering before you die and I can't wait that long, ho ho ho. Lots of good works to do. But don't worry, I'll be back before the end. My flunkies here will look in on you every few days. Exit, cape swirling." I looked up, panting from all the typing, my fingers sore. "How's that?"

She snorted. "'Twill serve." She exited, cape swirling.

Only after the door had clicked shut did I dare sag, limp in my seat. "Crap."

CM pointed a long, crimson nail at me. "Don't start that again!" She looked around, listened to complete silence. "Great. Now what? All your characters are out getting ready to sue you or flay you alive, but your deadline's getting no farther away."

"Don't worry," I said, sorting the Enchantress' new pages, "There's another character I can work on." Now where was the rest of this story?

CM looked around, just like I was, but for something else. "Who? Where? There's no one else—"

"She's doing a remote," I explained. Ah, there it was, under the pizza box.

CM frowned, trying to puzzle it out. "She? Remote?" Then she pointed at me again, an expression of triumph on her face. "You mean the—"

"What the hell is *this*?" It sounded like my voice, but it was so far away.

CM looked from my face to the pages I held, nearly crushing them. "What's what?" She craned her neck awkwardly to see, but I threw them down first.

"I don't write crap like that!" I shouted, standing, putting as much distance between myself and those pages as I could.

"No, but I do," shouted a voice, just as the door crashed open yet again. A portly, balding figure, clad in whatever black clothes he could find at local garage sales, redolent with Romano cheese and tomato sauce.

"*Reader's Rep*?!"

"Ha, ha," he chortled, "No longer will I be pushed aside, trampled by the unworthy. I will have my rightful place! I am Reader's Rep, everyone's underling, no more! You may call me—" he paused dramatically "—*Dark* Reader's Rep!"

Oh, God!

"Now there's a guy who could use a creative muse," observed CM snidely.

"Help, oh help," I said softly, deadpan. "Where is a hero when you need one?" I took a sip of my soda and raised my eyebrows at her, questioningly.

She stuck her tongue out at me, her hand doing a seesaw motion in the air. "The right cliché," she admitted. "But the pizza had better delivery."

"Silence, trollop!" bellowed Rea—*Dark* Reader's Rep, pointing a finger at her. I expected her to take it off, preferably at the elbow, but she just sat there smirking at him. That was probably worse. She's so smart.

Finding no easy target there, he turned to me. "You lose, Author Guy! I slunk in here, all whipped and downtrodden, and stole your story away from you, right under your nose. With my pages in place, salability will increase a hundredfold."

I was incredulous. "That bilious tripe? A woman in a dungeon six months, yet her hair still flowed and billowed over high, pert breasts? What kind of swill do you think my readers will swallow?"

"They're *my* readers now, Author Guy, and they'll take whatever swill I throw at them, as long as there's breasts in it." He picked up my neat and orderly manuscript, getting greasy fingerprints all over it. "Look at this junk. No blood and guts anywhere, just wit and repartee. Where's the gore? Where's the screaming and moaning? Where's the heavy breathing? Where's—"

"WHERE'S THAT AUTHOR CREEP?!" someone screamed from just without, as the door crashed in yet again. Good thing I had the wall reinforced, but even so...

I goggled. "Loretta?" She was practically falling out of her clothes, but I knew better than to look. Fortunately she has very interesting feet.

She pounced, grabbing me by the collar and pounding my head against the wall. "Look what you did to me!" I took one quick glance, as directed—spectacular—and jerked my eyes heavenward once again.

"Not me," I choked. "Him." I pointed at Read—*Dark Reader's Rep.*

She turned her furious face on him and dropped me, finding in his leering face and drool complete confirmation of my words. He rubbed his hands lasciviously, looking her over like a display. "Now isn't that the nicest sales figure I ever saw! You got the cover, baby," the fool gloated, not recognizing his danger.

I did, and I scrambled to hide under the desk, but CM was already there. "That *is* Loretta, right? The greatest DiD in print?"

I nodded. "Yeah, but that idiot made her a '*Delicious* Damsel in *Dire* Distress'."

She understood immediately, and hunkered down smaller. "Oh my god." I could hear the awe mingling with terror in her voice.

"That's right. He slapped double D's on her without even asking." It takes a special woman to be a Damsel in Distress, and DRR was finding out *how* special. 'Never mess with the Damsel in Distress', as the saying goes. We didn't want to see it, so we kept our eyes shut. I can sit and listen to mayhem for hours, it's pretty much what I do, but when he started screaming it was more than even I could take. I reached up, feeling around the top of my desk for the offending pages, and tossed them on the floor. Not only is that where they belonged, it's where he was. "Run, you fool!" I screamed, "Run for your life!"

There was a sound of whimpering desperation, a grunt as even Loretta was pushed away, and the clatter of boot heels as the villain fled.

"Is it safe?" I called, eyes still shut.

A hand tapped my knee. "Come on out," said Loretta, "It's all right now."

We clambered out, a little stiff from the cramped quarters, and Loretta's hand was rock-steady as she helped us to our feet. I barely glanced at her—her waist is so narrow—before turning away so fast I gave myself whiplash. "Wow," said CM, behind me. "That sure gives a new meaning to 'bodice-ripper.'"

There was a sound of fumbling. "Oh, he didn't touch me," she said, a little muffled. "Okay, you can turn around now, Author Guy." She was wearing a new shirt, of course, something of CM's. I checked out the old one. Most of the seams were intact, but the fabric had split in several places. "Most of that was from the—you know—" she put her hands up, pulled them away quickly, indicating the explosive expansion she had undergone "—and me hanging from the ceiling—" she fixed an unpleasant glare on me "—waiting around for a *very long time*, I thought. And it threw me off balance, being top-heavy like that, so I had to get one of the flunkies to let me down. And of course they all had gone to lunch, expecting me to get myself down, so I was calling and yelling practically forever, like I was some kind of damsel in distress! A thing like that can ruin a girl's rep."

"Not when I get through with it," I promised, feeling noble.

"You'd better," she declared. With CM backing her up, I felt a good bit less noble. *Now, how to begin...*

"Okay, how's this: Damsel dangles from ceiling, diaphanous gown, billowing hair, high, pert breasts, all that stuff. Flunky comes in to leer. 'Please sir, if you'd let me down I'd be ever so grateful.' Flunky complies, leering more. Delicate, sylph-like thing, no threat, have my lecherous way with her. Damsel wraps chains around flunky's neck, leaps into pit, so long flunky. Damsel climbs up, gets keys, steals knife, goes off looking for trouble. The best man for the job is a woman. Wanna get it done right, gotta do it yourself." I smiled up at their less-unhappy faces. "You like?"

Loretta nodded. "It'll do." Turning to CM, she said, "I'll see you later. I'm gonna go off and kill somebody."

CM tousled her billowing, flowing hair. "That's the spirit. Go get 'em."

As she left, I feared for the safety of the civilized world.

Then I noticed the wreck of my office. "Dammit. All that bitching about her tough-girl reputation, you think she'd clean up after herself, but *noooo*—"

CM found an uneaten crust, righted a chair and sat down. "Speaking of bitching..."

"I am not bitching!"

"No, I meant, here comes Fearless Hero back again." She stuck the crust in her mouth and waited.

The door opened. Gently. FH, stood there, a little downcast. "Author Guy, it appears I owe you an apology." He looked unhappy; I'm sure he would much rather have run me through.

I relaxed in my chair. "How so?"

He closed the door, and stood at rest, the point of his sword digging a hole in my floor as his hands lay crossed on the pommel. He grimaced and said, "My union rep has informed me that—that it is not the words we say but the actions we undertake which prove our worth."

Somehow I found that hard to believe. "Did he really?"

"No," FH confessed, reddening. "He said 'Dialog, schmialog, just go beat up the bad guys.'"

That sounded more like it.

"Would you like some bad guys to beat up on, is that it?"

He was relieved that he did not have to ask. "If you would."

I hid my grin— "Be a pleasure."—until I spun in my chair, and flashed it at CM. We'll make that deadline yet! I quickly re-read my pages. "Hmm, slight problem here."

"What is it now?" he asked resignedly, and I explained about EE's magic chains. "Quite the clever scheme, writer. How am I to save myself?"

"Easy," I said breezily, making it up as I went along, "Flexing your mighty wrists, you pull the links taut against the manacles, which grip the final links of the chain, making the chain razor-sharp against the manacles, and working tirelessly, you rub the chain against the manacles until it cuts through, leaving your hand free. In no time you free your other limbs, and head for the door. In spite of you being hopelessly shackled, they locked it anyway, which forces you to alert the guards by breaking it down. You slay the first with your bare hands, take his sword, and starting hacking your way to freedom." I looked up at his satisfied grin. "Go get 'em."

CM smiled, but said nothing.

"I go, good author," he boomed, whipping out his sword. I opened the door, before he cut a hole in it, and he was off.

"'Have at thee, knaves.' 'Have AT thee, knaves!'" His voiced trailed away, still practicing. I closed the door, and turned to find CM staring at her watch. With her other hand she was counting off 5, 4, 3, 2 and pointed to the door just as—

Wham! Evil Enchantress stood there, panting heavily, which would have been an enjoyable sight except for the smoke and sparks. "You win, author guy, so you'd better make this good."

"Ah!" I smirked, "So your rep—"

"It said, 'Character, schmaracter, as long as you kill a lot of people.'" She leaned in close, and I coughed on the fumes. "Who do I kill? For the greater good, of course," she added, in an off-hand way. Gotta hand it to her, she sure can roll with the punches.

"Um," I temporized hastily. "Let me check the play list." Which was short, and right on top, dammit. "Uh, well, let's see, the Hero's free— "

"Can I kill him?" she asked, her eyes gleaming.

"With what? Even the Damsel in Distress is cutting through your flunkies."

We all had the same thought. "Cool," she breathed heavily. "If I have to kill my own flunkies, it's one of those little sacrifices we have to make, and it cleanses the gene pool of incompetence."

"Even better," added CM. "You do it by releasing your priceless collection of hideously dangerous rare beasts. Can't let endangered species be harmed, now can you?"

EE giggled. "You've still got it!"

I shook my head as they congratulated each other. "You guys are so mean."

They both turned to stare at me. "To flunkies? It's what they're for!" said CM.

EE agreed, adding, "Please. They grow 'em in vats."

"And besides," CM continued, throwing her crust at me, "it's not like *we're* the ones writing this stuff, so don't get all innocent with *us*!"

Maybe so, but I was just as glad neither of these two were at my back at that moment. Anyway, to business. "Okay, a bunch of horrible deaths, coming right up," I declared, cracking my fingers dramatically. "Let's see, Fearless Hero hacking and slashing from below, Distressed Damsel slicing and dicing from above. Blood flowing in rivers, 'help, help, Mistress, save us!' 'Save yourselves fools, or cleanse the gene pool with your blood...'"

"Ooh, I like that!" enthused EE, clapping.

"Told you," murmured CM, stealing my drink. She really was evil.

"'Hard times call for harsh measures. The Cause's need is great, your squeamishness only sickens me. Get out!'" I paused for breath, fingers tiring. "Give me back my drink. Your plots are ruined, your apparatus smashed—"

"What apparatus?"

"Who cares, it's smashed. But you'll get them, at least. Too bad about the flunkies, but the devoted ones will be glad to make the ultimate sacrifice for the greater good, the undevoted ones are no loss—"

"Logic-chopping 101. Took it in my junior year," said CM, smugly.

"'Silence, troilop.' But the beasts in your care, the endangered species so close to extinction, must not be harmed so you let them all go, who cares if they're all poisonous man-eaters? Man isn't an endangered species and they are. Now pull that lever, the castle will come down in nine minutes, that way the heroes can escape for the sequel while still creating a false feeling of suspense. 'I'll get you yet!' Exit, cape swirling. Castle comes crashing down just minutes later, lots of dust and booming noises, no sign of hero or damsel." I sprang back from the keyboard, flopped in my chair, panting exaggeratedly, apparently oblivious to the whistling and applause.

I heard a shuffle and looked up. EE was standing, addressing an imaginary audience, "I'd like to thank my author, his muse, and of course all the flunkies whose grisly and horrible deaths made this moment possible—"

I threw the crust at her, but she blasted it before it connected. "Oh, hush, you've got the sequel," I told her, getting up to steal my drink back before CM finished it on me.

"Well, of course, foolish mortal," she cooed. "Who else?" She blew me a kiss, and headed for the hallway. "I'll just go pack up my snakes. Give me a call when you're ready. It's been fun."

CM waited until even the foul smell of her perfume had cleared the room. "'Who else?'" she echoed, not quite loudly enough to be heard outside the room. "I could be more evil than her while half asleep. My *snores* are more evil than hers."

I put a finger to her lips, achieving a precious moment of silence. "I know," I said. "That's why you're a creative muse and her castle just self-destructed."

The moment lasted just long enough for me to reach my chair. "She can't really think she'll win a mystery for that," said CM, wiping water from her fingers. "They don't give trophies to also-rans."

Speeches and trophies I could put together, but—"What the hell is a 'mystery?' Aside from how you stay so thin, that is."

CM looked longingly at the pizza box, but turned away and sat primly. "That's 'Mister EEs', the award given for the most evil acts in a given year."

"EEs?"

"Evil Encarnate," she explained.

"That's *In*carnate," I corrected, ever punctilious.

"Oh, they know," she tossed off with a flip of her hair. "They just call it that to annoy you writer types."

Now I understood. Sort of. "You don't think she'll win?" I gestured vaguely towards the locker room door, keeping my voice low.

She shrugged. "Not the main award, with her castle in ruins," she stated definitively. "Maybe the Flair award, but they don't give that one anymore."

I knew I was going to regret asking, but— "Why not?"

"No presenters. They're too good at hiding." She finally gave in, reached for the box, but her wishy-washiness went unrewarded.

I blocked the box, as it sailed across the room, before it hit my head. "Do I want to know?"

She pretended to consider. "Do you like grotesque and occasionally gruesome acts? The Flair award is a bit of an insult."

I stared at her, realizing she was serious, and smiled weakly. "I don't want to know."

She smiled at me, and I took the moment to take a sip from my watery drink, icy and thin. It was almost a perfect interlude. Almost.

"By the way," she said. "How did your hero and damsel get out?"

"Oh. Didn't I tell you?"

Crash! Wham! Splinter! The door, so long abused, gave up at last and sagged off its hinges. Fearless Hero's foot, the source of the explosion, followed it through the doorway and came to rest upon its buckled corpse. FH himself came next, of course, all the mighty, bulging mass of him, teeth no longer shining, hair no longer flowing but matted and stringy with the blood of scores of unknown flunkies, his sword out and looking for at least one more victim. I was glad my stout writing desk was between—

SLICE!

—*had been* between us.

"You!" he roared, pointing at me with something far more dangerous than a finger. "This time I *will* kill you, and to hell with my union rep!"

I took a deliberately insolent sip from my drink, and handed it back to CM, still just sitting there on my couch. "Why, Fearless," I began, smiling brightly. "Is something wrong?"

"Saved by the Damsel?!"

CM exploded in mirth, spraying diluted soda all over the room. FH was gentleman enough to wait for her to stop coughing, while I stole that precious instant to hit one of the speed dial buttons on my phone. Finally he continued, "What makes you think I'll put up with this—this—"

"Crap?" supplied my muse.

"Don't you start!" His sword actually started to move in her direction.

I grabbed the blade—by the flat, of course—and pulled it back towards me, as if I were some kind of hero. "Look, Fearless," I said, ignoring the blade. "Do you want in on the sequel or not?"

The sword arm relaxed slightly. "Sequel?"

I snorted. "Of course, the sequel. Everything's sequels these days." I turned my back on his naked steel, rummaged in a drawer for some boilerplate. Ah, here we are. "You want in or not?" I handed over the contract.

He looked at the standard form dubiously, flicked eyes up at me. "No more rescues by the DiD?"

I sighed. "If you insist." I took the form back and wrote the addendum on the bottom, with my initials. "Happy?"

"Better." He signed.

I took back the form, stuck it in my drawer. "I'll get right on this, as soon as we get back from vacation."

"Vacation? Who is 'we?'" His eyes slid over to CM, who was looking demure.

I looked at her, chaos in bright clothes. "Good God, no."

She sniffed, turned her head up and above such things. "As it happens," she informed us both archly, "this is our last collaboration. I'm going back to grad school. There's an opening in the Junior Editors program."

"Really? Congratulations," I said, meaning it completely. With her off my couch maybe I could get some work done. "I'm sure you'll do fabulously. All the best Editors started out as Evil Enchantresses." FH gave her a gentlemanly kiss on the hand; mine was on her cheek. She really was a good CM.

"Now then, good author," said FH, turning to me once more. "What of this highly suspicious and conveniently-timed vacation?"

He was answered by a discreet tap on the doorframe, since there was nothing left to go 'wham' with anymore. "Hope I'm not interrupting."

FH goggled. "Loretta?" He'd never seen her like this before, in her civvies and quite so…big. Even CM was speechless.

"Hey baby," I said, carefully doing my best sexist-pig impression. "Even better than your cover art." She walked up to me and took my hand, smiled serenely at the others.

"He's consoling me," she informed them brightly. "The traumatic events of the lest few pages have left me feeling humiliated, abused, and overwrought. So he's taking me to Barbados for a couple of weeks, until I feel up to the pressures of the job again." She squeezed my hand, slightly, not quite enough to crumple steel, but close.

"A couple of weeks?!" FH was outraged. "What of the sequel? My reputation will be dogmeat by then. I should—"

Loretta forced his hand down without working up a sweat. "Listen, buddy," she said, loudly enough that even EE in the ladies' locker room could hear. "Nobody touches *my* author without going through *me* first! Got it?"

FH held out a hand, pleadingly. "But—"

"And if you think your rep's bad now, how about I tell some of the right people that your sword, your muscles, and your mouth are the biggest things about you, in that order. *Comprende*?!"

He turned bright red, head drooping. "Got it," he mumbled.

She put a finger under his chin, lifted his head up to look her in the eye. "It'll be okay, Fearless," she consoled him gently. "The women's groups'll love it, and when we get back, you can rescue me as many times as you want. Just tell 'em it's a career move."

He nodded dumbly a few times, reeled off and collapsed on my sofa.

"Are we all off then?" I asked, looking around. Two satisfied female faces assured me that we were. "Let's get going. CM, we'll drop you off on the way. Oh, and Fearless, when the crew comes to fix my door, just let 'em in, okay? They already know the make, model, color, size, address, and my account number." I go through a lot of doors.

He didn't bother to look up, just gestured appropriately.

"Thanks. Bye, then." And I left, whistling. I love happy endings.

* * *

Fearless Hero lifted his head, gazed upon the carnage that had once been a peaceful author's studio. Now it was Hell, nor was he out of it.

"I'll get him," he swore silently, "I'll get him if it's the la—"

"I wouldn't finish if I were you," a female voice threatened in a lazy drawl. Evil Enchantress, her snakes and gossip bag completely packed, stood in the doorway.

FH was in no mood. "Or what, Witch? You'll poison my apples?"

"Worse," she sauntered over, placing her bag of writhing cobras right by his feet. "I'll sue you for copyright infringement. That's my line."

He leaned back on the couch, eyes up, intrigued by the pattern of cracks in the ceiling tiles. "Crap."

She sat next to him, slinkily, one hand drawing a teasing finger across his broad chest. "There, there, witchie will make it all better," she promised, rubbing portions of her anatomy against portions of his. "I'll make a villain of you yet, kid."

Hero rejected the very idea. His devotion to the powers of Light was as great as ever. But he wouldn't mind letting her try. "Curses," he said, trying to sound dispirited, "Foiled again."

About the Author:

Marc Vun Kannon earned a BA in philosophy and a wife from Hofstra University. He still has both, but the wife is more useful. He is currently working on his second BA in Computer Science. He feels that his real job is being a father to his three children, husband to his wife, and author to his books. He, and they, now reside in Wading River, Long Island, New York.

marcvunkannon@echelonpress.com
http://www.marcvunkannon.com

Printed in the United States
35179LVS00001B/85-111